The Siege
A Novel

by

Marilyn Baron

The Siege
A Novel

Cover Art by *Debbie Taylor*

The Wild Rose Press, Inc.
PO Box 708
Adams Basin, NY 14410-0708
Visit us at www.thewildrosepress.com

Publishing History
First Mainstream Women's Fiction Rose Edition, 2018
Print ISBN 978-1-5092-1863-9
Digital ISBN 978-1-5092-1864-6

Published in the United States of America

"Go back to your room," the American tour director ordered, shouting at the woman.

"I can't get the door to open," Theia protested, thrusting her key card at him in frustration.

The tour director hurriedly took the proffered card in sweaty hands and tried the lock, which didn't click. He jammed the key card into the slot again, to no avail.

A man opened the door and stuck his head out of the room. "What's wrong? Is this some kind of a fire drill?"

"It's no drill. Get back in your room and shelter in place until I give the all-clear. Don't open the door to anyone." The tour director returned Theia's card. "Get back in your room with your husband."

"This is my room, but he's not my husband," Theia insisted.

"There must be some kind of mistake," the man in the room announced. "This is *my* room."

The tour director grabbed the woman's key card again and examined the key holder. He shook his head, rolled his eyes, and looked at Theia like she was a recalcitrant child. "You're on the wrong floor, miss. This is Room 515. You're in Room 415."

"I'm sorry." Theia blew out a breath and turned to leave. The tour director blocked her way.

"Excuse me, but I need to get back to my room." Tears of exhaustion pooled in her eyes. She wanted to scream.

"I'm afraid you can't go anywhere. We've disabled the elevators for your safety, and hotel security is blocking the stairs, for now." He ushered her into Room 515 and pushed her into the arms of the man standing at the door.

Praise for Marilyn Baron

"Marilyn Baron's *STUMBLE STONES* grabbed me from the start with its opening hook... *STUMBLE STONES*, named so for the plaques laid in tribute to victims of the Holocaust, possesses the best qualities of historical romance. Baron knows her settings and her history, and her characters, those both contemporary and in the past, are well-drawn and convincing. Baron has a great talent for dialogue, both in the banter of her modern lovers, as well as those engaged in much more serious conversations in the novel's past narrative."

~Georgia Author of the Year Judge

"*THE ALIBI* is an unfolding of a tale filled with Southern, small town mystery, intrigue, suspense, murder, and a bit of down home charm. [It] is humorous, shocking, downright scandalous in a small town sort of way, and an absolute enjoyable read."

~Gabrielle Sally, The Romance Reviews (5 Stars)

"Baron has a compelling and entertaining story that will leave readers craving more of these characters' lives! ...a superb job with character development and credibility. As this mystery slowly unfolds, so many things are thrown at these characters in rapid succession—making the story fun and enticing! If you are a reader of mystery, suspense, and crime fiction, you may want to pick this up!"

~Turning Another Page, Book Unleashed (5 Stars)

"Marilyn Baron brings a unique style to her quirky and fast-paced stories that keeps readers turning pages."

~New York Times Bestseller Dianna Love

"A treasure trove of mystery and intrigue...."

~Andrew Kirby

Dedication

To the Jews of Crete and Rhodes who perished
in the Holocaust,
and to what might have been.
To those who survived, and the next generations.

The *Tanais* Tragedy:
What Happened to the Jews of Crete

On the morning of May 29, 1944, the two hundred and sixty-five Jews of Crete, along with some Christian resistance fighters and Italian prisoners, were rounded up and arrested by German occupying forces in the old Jewish quarter. They were herded together and transferred into a convoy of trucks, taken to Ayias Prison, located not far from Chania (Hania), Crete's second largest city, where they were kept in inhuman conditions.

On the moonlit night of June 8, 1944, they were transferred to Heraklion, the largest city on the island of Crete, and herded into the cargo hold of the *Tanais*, a requisitioned merchant vessel sailing in a convoy to Piraeus (Athens). There they would have joined Jews from Corfu and Zakynthos, headed by train for the concentration camp at Auschwitz.

At 2:31 a.m., on June 9, thirty-three miles northeast of Heraklion, off the island of Santorini, the *Tanais* was sighted by the British submarine *HMS Vivid.* At 3:12 a.m., the submarine fired two torpedoes and sank the ship within fifteen minutes, wiping out almost the entire Jewish population of Crete: the Jews and all aboard in its hold went down to a watery grave. Of the hundreds of victims, more than one hundred were children.

There was no counterattack. Wreckage was sighted—fifteen floating pieces of wood of various shapes and sizes and twelve forty-gallon oil drums, probably fuel.

For several years, there was a debate surrounding what caused the *Tanais* to sink. Many people believed that the Germans had sunk the ship themselves, to exterminate the Jewish hostages. The Germans always kept the cargo of their convoys a closely guarded secret, so the British wouldn't have known the Jews were aboard. The Allied Command regularly made indiscriminate attacks on all German and Italian convoys.

At least 60,000 of Greece's total pre-war Jewish population perished. Approximately twenty-five Cretan Jews outlived the war. Several evaded the roundup immediately before the deportation, and others, members of the 5th Cretan Division, did not return to the island. Today, there are only a dozen Jews left in Crete.

Part One
The Siege

"In our life there is a single color, as on an artist palette which provides the meaning of life and art. It is the color of love."

~Marc Chagall

Chapter One

Florence, Italy

"Shelter in place. Shelter in place! Lock your doors and shelter in place. Stay away from the windows!" A man's panicked voice, a horseless Paul Revere, harbinger of a coming invasion, echoed down the long, carpeted hallway of the Hotel Dei Fiori in Florence, as Theia Constas, dead on her feet, tried her room key for the second time.

"Go back to your room," the American tour director ordered, shouting at the woman.

"I can't get the door to open," Theia protested, thrusting her key card at him in frustration.

The tour director hurriedly took the proffered card in sweaty hands and tried the lock, which didn't click. He jammed the key card into the slot again, to no avail.

A man opened the door and stuck his head out of the room. "What's wrong? Is this some kind of a fire drill?"

"It's no drill. Get back in your room and shelter in place until I give the all-clear. Don't open the door to anyone." The tour director returned Theia's card. "Get back in your room with your husband."

"This is my room, but he's not my husband," Theia insisted.

"There must be some kind of mistake," the man in

the room announced. "This is *my* room."

The tour director grabbed the woman's key card again and examined the key holder. He shook his head, rolled his eyes, and looked at Theia like she was a recalcitrant child. "You're on the wrong floor, miss. This is Room 515. You're in Room 415."

"I'm sorry." Theia blew out a breath and turned to leave. The tour director blocked her way.

"Excuse me, but I need to get back to my room." Tears of exhaustion pooled in her eyes. She wanted to scream.

"I'm afraid you can't go anywhere. We've disabled the elevators for your safety, and hotel security is blocking the stairs, for now." He ushered her into Room 515 and pushed her into the arms of the man standing at the door. "You need to stay here until we get this all sorted out."

"But this is not my room!"

The tour director's patience was wearing thin. "I don't have time to explain, but you can't move now!" He started to pull the door closed.

"Wait," said the man in Room 515, trying to cope with a handful of seriously steamed woman. "What's going on here?"

Other heads appeared out of other doors down the hall, setting off a buzz of concern.

"Is something wrong?"

"What's all this racket about?"

"What's happening?"

"Is there a fire?"

"We have a *situation*," explained the frustrated tour director, his face growing progressively redder and his voice more strained. "You need to stay in your rooms and lock your doors until you receive further instructions."

"But we were just going down to the dining room," protested a man in a dinner jacket, heading out of his room, followed by his well-dressed wife, who was decked out in an impressive array of jewels.

"Stop," yelled the tour guide, raising his hand in front of his face.

How could those people eat? Theia wondered. When she got to her room, she was going to shed her clothes, plop face down on the mattress, and zonk out for the rest of the evening. And dream about soaking her feet in a hot tub, which she would totally do, if she could actually summon the strength to climb into the tub. The full-day tour to Cinque Terre had been like a forced death march.

The tour director glared at the complaining couple emerging from Room 517.

He barked a staccato-like warning that brooked no dissent. "Do. Not. Come. Down. To the dining room!" Then he ran down the hall toward the stairwell, issuing a final order as an afterthought before he disappeared. "And don't panic!"

The buzz continued, but within minutes, doors shut, locks clicked, and the hallway was silent as a darkened cemetery.

"Don't panic?" Theia repeated incredulously, shaking her head. "He practically threatens us and then he says, 'Don't panic'?"

She stood face-to-face with a tall, dangerously handsome stranger, who looked to be about thirty, blocking her way into the room—apparently, *his* room. As soon as she noticed his Aryan blond hair and blue eyes, she dismissed him. His traditional good looks might as well be a neon sign flashing *Not My Type*.

"The tour director just pushed me in here," she said flatly, stating the obvious.

"It's okay," the man in the room said calmly, unhanding the struggling girl. "You're welcome to stay until this, whatever this situation is, is over."

She looked beyond the man and around the room. It was more of a suite, if she was going to be literal, obviously much larger than hers, featuring a separate living area with a Mediterranean décor. She took in the ceiling beams, skylights, large picture window, and balcony. Besides the elephant in the room, the giant king-sized bed, there was a lot to focus on. She stared suspiciously at the man in front of her.

What if he's a terrorist?

"Don't worry. I'm not a terrorist."

"Why did you say that?"

"Because you just asked if I was a terrorist."

I said that out loud? I must really be exhausted. "I don't even know you."

"We're in the same tour group. You sat next to me on the bus today on the Cinque Terre excursion."

Theia stared at him blankly. "Well, I don't remember you."

The man shrugged. "I get that a lot. I seem to have that effect on women. Look, Miss Always Bringing Up the Rear, I'm exhausted. My feet hurt. I wasn't even going down to dinner. I need to rest."

"Bringing up the rear? What do you mean by that?" Theia demanded.

"On the excursion today, you were the perpetual straggler. The other people on the tour nicknamed you 'the Trailer.' "

Theia frowned. "I twisted my ankle on the cobblestones. I was having trouble walking."

"If you remember, I tried to help you, and you blew me off. I think your exact words were, 'I don't need your help. I work out.' Although I don't know what working out has to do with anything. I should have run in the opposite direction. You have some mouth on you." He stared at the mouth of his unwilling guest unflinchingly until she looked away.

"I'm leaving. I don't need to be insulted in my own room."

The man chuckled, revealing his dimples, which just served to infuriate her. "It's not your room now, is it? And you're not going anywhere." He pulled her farther into the room by the shoulders, led her over to a desk chair, and plopped her down into it. Then he went back to lock the door and latch it.

Theia pouted and folded her arms across her chest before making her pronouncement. "I don't want to be here."

"That makes two of us. I'd rather be enjoying a nice meal downstairs in the dining room. Or a good soak in a hot tub. But I don't have the strength to move, let alone eat or bathe. You heard what the tour director said. We don't have a choice. There's some kind of situation, and we are supposed to stay right here until it's resolved. It sounded serious."

"Do you always do what you're told? Yes, of course you do. You look like the type who always follows orders."

"Typically, that's the best course of action. Following the rules usually produces the most positive outcomes."

Theia looked at him like he had two heads. "I want to go to bed."

The man indicated the bed beside her. "Be my guest." He hesitated. "Look, we may as well get to know each other, if we're going to be stuck here. My name is Wade, by the way. Wade Bingham."

"Wade in the Water…" She began singing the familiar spiritual in a deep bass tone.

"That's hardly original. I've only heard it a billion times. And what's wrong with my name?"

"You have to admit Wade sounds sort of stuffy. Sorry. I guess I'm a little nervous."

"And cranky," Wade added.

"Okay, and cranky. I'm Theia Constas." She reached out her hand. He shook it.

Wade walked over to the window.

"What are you doing?" she asked, close on his heels. "The tour director said to stay away from the windows."

"I need to find out what's going on."

"Do you always disobey instructions?"

He rolled his eyes. "Make your mind up. Am I obedient or disobedient?"

"Sorry, I'm so tired I can't think straight. Can you see anything?" she asked anxiously, creeping up behind him.

"I don't want to go all the way out onto the balcony."

"What do you see out there?" Theia pressed, inching toward the window when all she wanted to do was collapse on the bed.

"A bunch of men dressed in black, wearing hoods

and carrying automatic weapons—AK-47s, I think—and black flags. But it's getting dark. I can't count how many people there are. There are some bodies on the ground. I didn't hear any shots." He pulled the drapes closed.

Theia shivered. "Are you saying there really are terrorists outside our hotel? How can this happen in Italy?"

"Don't you read the newspapers or watch the news? It can happen anywhere. It *is* happening everywhere. They could already be inside the hotel."

"What are we going to do?" Theia twisted the straps of her cross-body bag nervously.

"There's nothing we can do but wait."

"Wait to be blown up or shot or beheaded…or worse?"

"What's worse than being beheaded? Don't get ahead of yourself."

"I can't help it." Theia paced the room. Then she plopped back into the desk chair. "Patience isn't one of my strong suits."

"I noticed. This is an unusual situation."

"You're pretty zen about the whole thing."

"I'm an actuary."

Theia burst out laughing. "I would have guessed you were an underwear model. Figures I'd get stuck in a room with an actuary. I couldn't get trapped with a soldier or a cop or a secret agent or a bodyguard? Or at least a super hero?"

"I create a hell of a spreadsheet. I 'Excel' in other areas also."

Theia narrowed her straight, feathery brows.

"A little actuarial humor."

"Exactly what does an actuary do?"

"I review the amount of money insurance companies and large self-insured companies have saved up to pay for future insurance claims. And then I say whether or not the amount they have reserved is reasonable."

"Can you be more specific?"

"Take one of those huge soft drink companies. They have so many trucks and so many employees, it's much cheaper for them to insure their vehicles by themselves than it is for them to hire an insurance company, which would charge them a ton of money to pay all their claims, and they can have more control if they just do it themselves. A company like that has trucks all over the country and every day, probably, one of their trucks gets in an accident and they have to deal with that. Since they're self-insured, they have to pay money out to settle all of these claims. So what I do, when I'm auditing the balance sheets of one of those companies, is to calculate the amount of money they have to put away for a claim. But that's just an educated guess. If you get in an accident with one of that company's trucks, you could guess how much it would end up costing, but you wouldn't know right away. I have to determine what's legally required to put up money to protect against that. My job is to make sure they have the money put up to pay for future claims."

"I'll bet you could calculate the odds of us getting out of this hotel in one piece."

"I probably could, but I'd prefer not to. Let's look on the bright side."

"The bright side?" Theia posed, her voice growing more agitated. "What bright side?"

"The mini-bar is fully stocked, they refill it daily, and it's complimentary."

"Great. That makes me feel so much better."

"And speaking of the mini-bar, let's get some ice on that ankle." Wade went to the closet and grabbed a plastic laundry bag, filled it with ice, wrapped it in a hand towel, and walked over to Theia's chair. He lifted her foot gently and placed it on an ottoman. He pressed the ice packet gingerly against her sore ankle.

"Oh, that feels better," Theia sighed, shivering. Whether it was from his touch or the ice, she couldn't say. "Thank you."

"You're welcome."

"My point about the mini-bar is that if we're stuck in this room for more than a day, we'll need to eat. I doubt if they'll have room service. Like I said, I didn't have dinner tonight."

"Neither did I. I want to go home."

"Well, Dorothy, we're not in Kansas anymore, or wherever you're from. We're in Florence, Italy, so your ruby slippers don't work here."

Theia rolled her eyes. "Gee, why didn't I think of that? If I only had a brain."

Wade hovered over her chair. "Instead of sniping at each other, let's focus on the positive. We're alive, we're safe, for the time being, and we have a place to sleep. We're not out on the street."

"How can you sleep at a time like this?"

"Because that damn tour director walked our asses off today. I'm craving a hot shower, but I'm too tired to get undressed. And who knows? Those might be Italian police out there ready to rescue us. I'm going to conk out if I don't get into bed. Then I won't be of use to anybody."

"You are honestly going to sleep tonight?" Theia repeated.

"Hell, yes. I'm sure the Italian police have been called and this thing will be all over by tomorrow morning."

Theia's phone buzzed. She pulled it out of her purse, which she'd placed in the chair with her. "It's a text from my mother. She wants to know if I'm all right. She tried calling my room and there was no answer. She said there's a hostage situation at our hotel. It's all over the news. Let's turn on CNN or SKY News."

"Good idea." Wade walked over to the TV and turned it on.

"…hostage situation at the Hotel Dei Fiori in Florence, Italy. Carabinieri confirm five dead. The Italian military police report that an unknown number of terrorists are holding hostages in the hotel dining room…"

"I could have been in that dining room," Theia exclaimed.

"I know. That's where I was headed if I could have taken another step."

"CNN sources say the terrorists are threatening to kill hostages on live television."

Theia began to shake. Wade pressed a comforting hand on her shoulder. "We're safe in here. We're not in the dining room. So let's get comfortable and get ready for bed."

"Bed?"

"Yes," Wade said softly. "Sleep. We'll need our sleep if we're going to make rational decisions. You're halfway to delirious. You can hardly keep your eyes open. So come on. Up you go." Wade pulled her up gently by the hands and led her over to the bed. When she refused to budge, he lifted her and tried again. "Upsy-daisy."

"Did you seriously just say 'upsy-Daisy'? Do you think I'm a child?"

"Well, if you're not, then don't act like one. And look here, you do need a nap."

"Do you actually think I'm going to sleep with you? A total stranger?"

"I'm not propositioning you. I'm offering you a place to sleep. The bed is plenty big enough for both of us. Think of it as a slumber party."

"I don't have any PJs."

"It's a good thing I'm an underwear model. Free undergarments, one of the perks of the profession. You can wear one of my T-shirts." Wade went to his suitcase on the portable luggage rack and pulled out an oversized T-shirt. "Here." He tossed it to her.

"You think you're funny?"

"I know I'm not. I'm an actuary. I've been told, by a long line of women, starting with my mother and my sisters, that I have no sense of humor."

"I didn't mean to be rude. Th-thanks. Turn around while I put it on."

Wade shook his head. "I'll do you one better. I'll retreat into the bathroom."

"Good."

Wade walked off, and Theia quickly shed her clothes down to her panties and changed into Wade's T-shirt.

"You can come out now," she said.

Wade came out of the bathroom wearing only his underwear.

Theia's hand flew to her mouth.

"What?"

She stabbed her finger in the air. "You're not wearing any clothes."

"I usually sleep in the nude. This is me being modest."

"You look like a big hairy wolf."

Wade blew out a breath. "Just crawl under the covers, Little Red Riding Hood, and hide your pretty little head if you don't like what you see."

The problem was she liked what she saw. A lot.

"You're staring," Wade said, his eyes twinkling.

"I am not," she lied. She was actually drooling.

There was a lot to like about Wade and his suite. And the fine Italian linens didn't hurt. The bed looked heavenly, and it was calling her name.

Wade repositioned the ice pack on Theia's ankle, elevated her foot on a pillow, covered her up with a scrumptious duvet with a Delft design, then walked to the other side of the bed and turned his body away from hers, toward the bathroom. "And I don't want to hear a peep out of you, miss."

"Okay. But I'm not going to sleep." How could she sleep when his half-naked hairy body had hovered only inches from hers when he'd affixed the ice bag? Then he'd practically covered her with his body when he tucked her in.

Wade shrugged. "Suit yourself."

Theia snorted.

"Just don't snore," he said.

"I don't snore!" she retorted.

"Oh, yeah, you do. Big time. You snore like a bear. I recorded it on my iPhone."

"You did what?" Theia turned and glared at him.

"You snored on the tour bus all the way from La Spezia back to the hotel. I tried to wake you up to see the Carrera marble quarries and the Leaning Tower of Pisa out of the bus window, but you were out like a light."

"I was not."

"Believe what you want. My eyes don't lie, and neither do my ears. I can play it back for you. It wasn't exactly a symphony."

"You're such a dork."

"Now you're speaking my language. Lights out," Wade announced.

"You sound like a camp counselor."

Wade raised his hands in surrender. "I guess I can't do or say anything right where you're concerned. I'm letting you crash in my room. You should be grateful."

"Grateful?" For a minute, Theia was silent. Not repentant. Silent. Furiously silent. "In case I do doze off, you'd better promise to wake me up," she demanded.

Wade executed a perfect salute. "Yes, ma'am. Anything else, your highness?"

She was right about him. He looked German.

"Stay on your side of the bed, Adolph."

"My name is Wade."

"Ha! Mr. Literal. Can't you take a joke?"

****

Adolph? What the hell was this woman ranting about? He was an American. His family was Swiss. All he'd done was give her a place to spend the night and

13

ice her ankle. He didn't have to do that. He could have left her stranded in the hall at the mercy of the terrorists, helpless, with that twisted ankle, like a wounded fawn. Could he help it if he was a gentleman? That he wanted to come to her rescue? Women! They were all nuts. He was raised in a house full of women, and he still couldn't understand them. He'd gotten out of his last relationship just in the nick of time.

What were the odds? He'd sat next to her on the coach on the tour to Cinque Terre. It had been a full and exhausting day. They'd enjoyed a scenic drive through the Tuscan countryside and traveled by boat to the five breathtaking villages nestled in steep cliffs along the Ligurian Sea. He had never seen such beauty except when he'd stolen furtive glances at the girl seated next to him on the bus.

There was that unforgettable lunch of *spaghetti con vongole* at a little café in Manarola, and the killer view as they left on the ferry to the next island. And the *stracciatella gelato* at the ice cream shop on Monterosso al Mare. When they were seated together at lunch, he pretended they *were* together. But she'd hardly said a word to him or anyone else. She spent the whole time rubbing her sore ankle. He would have gladly provided assistance, had they been properly introduced. But Miss Snooty Pants had made it clear she wanted nothing to do with him.

What Wade found most unforgettable about the excursion was the girl the rest of them had named "the Trailer" because she was always pulling up the rear. To be fair, there was a shitload of walking on that tour, and she was clearly not up to the task. The group had had to wait for her numerous times. At one point, she'd fallen so far behind they'd almost missed the train. Theia, the Trailer. He would definitely tease her about it later.

By the time they got off the bus in front of the hotel, she could hardly walk; her ankle was swollen to the size of a melon. He'd offered his hand when she was limping back to the hotel, but she refused it as she had refused any assistance during the grueling excursion. Stubborn little thing. She'd been asleep most of the way back, so he hadn't had an opportunity to talk to her, and he had a zillion questions. Where did she come from? What did she do for a living? Why was she here on this particular tour? How did she get the face of an angel? A face any Italian master would have killed to paint. Wearing an off-the-shoulder poplin top with a hint of bra showing, and a ruffled skirt, she was irresistible.

Being seated next to each other on the bus and in the restaurant gave him an opportunity to stare at her amazing face. The scenery paled in comparison. Of course she didn't notice him. He was invisible to most women. He even enjoyed listening to her snore, as she was snoring away, like a freight train, right now in bed next to him.

In his bed! How did he get so lucky? Fate had thrown them together, and he was not going to let this opportunity pass him by. What were the odds? Even though he was an actuary, pretty much of a numbers guy, he still believed in fate. There was a reason this woman had been put in his path. There must be. And he wasn't above taking advantage of the situation.

He studied his exotic bedmate in repose. She was some kind of Mediterranean mix, Spanish maybe, or Italian? Her name was unusual, too. It sounded Greek.

He'd looked it up on the Internet on his cell phone while she was asleep. In Greek mythology, Theia meant "goddess," or divine, daughter of the Earth and mother of the Sun, the Moon, and the Dawn. Appropriate. The kind of classic beauty you saw in fashion or movie magazines. Tall and lithe, she had a model's body with shoulder-length dark, wavy hair kissed with auburn streaks, and a dark complexion like she spent a lot of time in the sun. Dreamy green eyes, he knew, although they were shut now. A perfectly sculpted upturned nose, and well-defined cheekbones, and that endearing space between her two front teeth that made him want to press his lips against her kissable mouth and stick his tongue between them. A soft indention between the top of her lip that he wanted to press his thumb against. And a fleshy, suck-worthy lower lip she was biting in her sleep that was making him rock hard.

He'd first noticed her at the opening reception. She was stunning in an off-the-shoulder turquoise crepe dress. She wore her hair up so it looked short. He was happy to see it tumbling down the next day at the Uffizi Gallery. She was in a cherry print top and a cherry print ruffle skirt and wore sexy wraparound sandals that reminded him of Mercury. She kept to herself, mostly, entranced by the paintings, always with a sketchpad in hand. He had even seen her cry in front of one of them, the one where the goddess—Venus—rose out of the water on a half shell. He'd hardly listened to the guide. He couldn't take his eyes off the beauty that put Venus to shame.

She'd been entranced the previous day when the guide had shepherded them through scores of churches, from the Santa Maria Novella Church and the Church of Santa Croce to the Brancacci Chapel and the Baptistery of St. John, to view the frescoes, paintings, and other great Renaissance masterpieces.

She had practically drooled over the extraordinary view of Florence from the top of the Duomo. Well, it had been quite a view, and Theia had looked magnificent at sunset. He had the feeling she had done more than just tourist duty to check the churches off her bucket list. She was really into it. He was dying to see what was in her sketchpad. And when he had sneaked a peek while she was in the bathroom at a rest stop, he'd been pleasantly surprised to see a sketch of him. So, for all her feigned indifference, she had noticed him, too. Interesting.

She had valiantly tried to stay awake but had drifted off into slumber almost the moment her head hit the pillow. She looked great in his T-shirt. He was imagining what she might look like out of it. She had been sleeping on her fist, with her body crunched up into a ball. Now the covers that she'd kept pulled up to her chin in modesty had fallen down around her, and her magnificent body was unfurled like a flag, so he had an intimate, bird's-eye view of her long tanned legs and what he imagined were her pert breasts, not overripe but most likely a perfect fit for his hands, should he ever get lucky enough to touch them. He was smitten. There was no other word for what he felt. He was drawn to her like never before to any other woman. Not even his ex-fiancée.

Her lips were full, and his first instinct was to kiss them, but that would make him lower than low, taking liberties with, and advantage of, a half-naked woman who had wandered to his room mistakenly and ended up, through no fault of her own, in his bed.

Was he scared of the terrorists? Hell, yes. Who wouldn't be? Any minute they could be swarming the halls, breaking down doors, possibly shooting people and setting the hotel on fire. Or blowing it up. But he wasn't going to let Theia know his innermost fears. He would protect her, and part of his role was to keep her calm. He tried to stave off his fears and slow his heartbeat. But every time he looked at her, his heart galloped. He couldn't get his mind off her.

Reaching for his phone on the end table, he checked his CNN app. True to their threats, the terrorists had already executed two people, an elderly couple from Cincinnati, Ohio, who were taking the tour to celebrate their fiftieth anniversary. They were very sweet together. He had talked to them, and they told him they'd been together so long their children claimed they even snored in synchrony. They had held hands all day, on and off the bus, and he remembered thinking how lucky they were to have each other. He imagined having a life partner like that and growing old with someone like Theia. But the lucky couple was not so lucky tonight. They'd been beheaded on live TV, in the dining room in front of the rest of the hostages and the world. He wasn't going to share that horrifying news with Theia. She was at peace now, and he wanted her to stay that way. He didn't want to expose her to the evil in the world. How fortunate that he and Theia were not in the dining room.

He'd been getting frantic texts all night from his parents and his sisters and co-workers, who were worried sick about him. The terrorists had given another deadline and threatened to execute another two hostages if their demands weren't met. What were their demands? No one had yet claimed responsibility for the incident. The Italian police were on call but weren't making a move, in order to protect the hostages. Theia's phone had been buzzing all night.

The next morning, the sun crept into the room from behind the curtains, and Theia was snuggled up warmly against his body. He hesitated, but only for a second, and pulled her closer, reveling in her scent, enfolding her in his arms, pretending for a moment that she was aware of their intimacy and had invited it. Her kissable lips were dangerously close to his.

They were scheduled to leave on the high-speed train for Rome today and then go on to the Amalfi Coast, and Venice after that. But obviously the terrorists had thrown a wrench into those plans. He had hardly slept a wink last night, and he had the kinks in his neck and back to prove it. But it had been worth it to hold on to the priceless package, this sleeping goddess, in his arms. She was irresistible. And he never wanted to let her go.

Chapter Two

Theia's eyes flew open. Where was she? From the bright light spilling through the window, it was morning—somewhere. She was enfolded in a cloud of warmth, but the covers had been thrown off. She usually slept with the pet whale shark she'd purchased from the Georgia Aquarium, but the stuffed animal was nowhere in sight, and nothing about this room seemed familiar. Somebody's arms were banded possessively across her breasts. Her legs were bare, but that someone was radiating intense body heat. She was wearing a T-shirt that smelled of oak and musk. She wiggled her backside gently and burrowed back to the body warmth into what felt like—a giant erection. WTF?

She broke out of the embrace and swirled to face the man who had imprisoned her. Suddenly, she recalled agreeing to sleep in this bed, but not to—snatches of memory came tumbling back. Florence, Italy. Someone named Wade? And terrorists?

She bolted up in the bed.

"What is going on here?" Theia demanded, pointing an accusatory finger in Wade's face.

Wade surfaced from pseudo-sleep with a satisfied smile on his face.

"Hey," he said softly.

"Hey? Hey? Hay is for horses. What were you doing?"

"I was asleep," he said groggily, newly noting and appreciating Theia's faint Southern accent. Interesting. "I could use some coffee. I'll make us some."

"Hold on, there, mister. What were your arms doing on my breasts?"

Wade look confused. "Your breasts? I must have been dreaming."

"Then how do you explain that giant boner I just came up against?"

Wade flashed a sheepish grin. "I can't."

Theia jumped out of bed. "What am I doing in your T-shirt?"

"You didn't have any clothes."

"And why is that? What exactly is going on here?"

Wade sat up. "Don't you remember? I loaned you a T-shirt when we were stuck in this room together. You were trying to get back to your room, but you were on the wrong floor."

Indignant, Theia rose to gather her clothes and shoes from the chair. "Well, I'm going back there."

Wade pulled her against his body. "Hold on, there, Slim. You're not going anywhere. We have a situation here."

Theia reached for her cell phone and checked her messages. "My parents must have been calling all night."

"Do you remember anything about what happened last night?" Wade asked, holding her tighter as she wriggled against him, worried that she'd disintegrate into panic mode again; he'd barely gotten her calmed down last night, and now he was more worried that she'd leave his bed and his life forever.

"Between us?"

"I didn't take any liberties, if that's what you mean. Nothing happened between us, or I would have known about it." Wade sounded disappointed.

"What aren't you telling me?"

"Our hotel was surrounded by terrorists. It's all over the news. They've already executed that sweet elderly couple on our tour, the ones celebrating their fiftieth anniversary, dammit, and they're threatening to keep doing it. They may already have done it."

Theia shook. She slumped back against Wade's hard body. "How awful."

He continued to hug her tight. "It's going to be all right. I promise. I'll protect you."

Theia scratched her head and removed Wade's hands, which were wandering suspiciously close to her breasts again.

She turned to face him. "And just how are you going to do that? Do you happen to have a gun on you? Or are you going to bash them over the head with your calculator?"

"No, I don't have a gun," Wade answered evenly. "And actuaries don't use calculators. We use computers, but I didn't bring my computer on vacation with me. So I'm going to use my head. If I let you go, do you promise not to get hysterical or bolt?"

Theia folded her arms defiantly. "I am not hysterical. And as for bolting, what choice do I have?" Wade released her slowly.

She moved across the bed, grabbed her purse and clothes, and fled toward the bathroom, until she almost dropped to the floor in pain.

"My ankle," she cried out.

"It still hurts? Didn't the ice help? Do you need me

to come over there?"

"No. It feels a lot better, but—" She winced in pain. "I must have landed the wrong way when I jumped out of bed." She limped slowly to the bathroom, using the wall and the door for support. After she relieved herself, she studied her image in the mirror. Her hair was disheveled. Her makeup was smudged. It looked like she had—that they had—but that couldn't be. She would have remembered that. All she had were the clothes she had worn on the excursion yesterday, and they were all wrinkled, nasty-looking, and smelly, but she had no choice but to wear them again. Then she shifted her attention to the bathroom. The bathroom was amazing.

In fact, there were two bathrooms—one with a large rain shower head and the other with a hydro-massage bathtub for two and a private Jacuzzi. She could get used to this—premium vanity accessories and luxuriously fluffy, white, monogrammed towels. She showered with some fabulous Italian brand of shower gel and washed her hair under the rain shower, her tears mingling with the warm shower water while she shook, all the time worrying that a hooded terrorist would bang down the door and drag her naked body out, kicking and screaming. And do Lord knows what else to her.

Toweling off the tears, she dried herself and slipped on a white robe hanging on the back of the bathroom door, then sat at the vanity and began styling her hair with the hotel dryer. She had to compose herself before Wade saw her crying like a hysterical woman.

When she came out of the bathroom, she listened to a series of frantic messages from her parents that ended with, "Who is Wade?" Then she dialed her parents' number.

"Mom, Dad, I listened to your messages. Everything is okay. I'm okay."

"Who is Wade?"

"How did you hear about Wade?"

"He answered your phone last night. We wanted to talk to you, but he didn't want to wake you up." She knew they were wondering how she ended up in a man's bedroom in the middle of the night. She glanced over at Wade, who was sitting up on the bed. He must not have slept at all. He had monster-sized bags under his eyes. Even his bags had bags.

"Wade is a man in my tour group. I was standing outside his room by mistake when my tour guide pushed me in here so I wouldn't get caught in the hall."

"You spent the night in a stranger's hotel room?"

A stranger's bed. Leave it to my mother to worry about where I slept in the middle of a terrorist siege.

"He sounds older."

"He is," Theia admitted.

Then her mother asked the inevitable question. The question she had heard numerous times before.

"Is he Greek?"

"No, he's not Greek."

And the expected follow-up. The one-two punch.

"Is he Jewish, at least?"

"Hardly." *The blond hair and blue eyes were a dead giveaway.* "The furthest thing from." Would it have made a difference, if she'd slept in the bed of a Jewish Greek stranger? Probably. It certainly would have made the lapse more palatable to her parents.

"Mom, Dad, I think you're missing the point. I'm

not going to marry him. Terrorists have taken over the hotel, and I could have been killed. I could still be killed."

"We know," said her mother anxiously. "It's all over the news. They've threatened to kill another person. They've issued another ultimatum."

"Who are *they*?"

"No one has taken credit yet, but their methods have ISIS written all over them," her father interrupted. "The Italian authorities are stationed in the stairwells and outside the building, but they're afraid if they breach the dining room, more hostages may be killed. They're not sure if some of the terrorists might be holed up in other parts of the hotel. But Italian commandos are going through the hotel, room by room, to root them out and evacuate the…survivors. The FBI has a team on standby. We can see flames and smoke coming out of the windows."

"They've told us to stay in our rooms," Theia explained, sniffing the air for smoke.

"Then listen to them," her mother said. "But that didn't work out so well in the London fire. People were told to stay in place, and that was the wrong advice." That comment made Theia feel even worse. Now she was worried about Islamist terrorists possibly hiding out in a room down the hall and about a conflagration. "How long can this standoff last?"

Wade was accessing the Internet on his phone. "The terror siege in Mumbai, India, in 2008, lasted two and a half days."

Theia frowned. "Do you have to be so literal? That was a figurative question."

"Please keep in touch," her mother said. "I hate to

hang up. Do you want us to stay on the phone with you?"

"I'll be okay," Theia said. "I'm not alone."

"Please be careful, honey. We love you very much."

"I love you too." Theia hung up the phone.

"It says in this article that 195 people were killed and 295 wounded in the Mumbai attack," Wade continued.

"That doesn't make me feel any better. I shouldn't have slept last night."

"You were so exhausted, I don't think you could have stayed awake if you wanted to."

"Did you get any sleep last night?"

"I slept some this morning."

"What were you doing all night?"

Wade flashed a lopsided smile and shrugged his shoulders. "Watching you."

He scrolled down. "In Mumbai, the terrorists attacked other spots in the city before they attacked the hotel. I wonder if there were any other attacks reported in Florence, or if this is just the first wave."

"I wonder how many of them there are," Theia said.

"I don't know. There were about twelve in Mumbai."

Despite the drawn curtains, Theia could tell it was midmorning. She had an urge to look out the window.

"Let me do it," Wade said. He wandered over to the window and pulled the drapes. He opened the balcony doors.

Theia heard the sound of explosions and a hail of gunfire outside the hotel. She jumped back. "Do you smell smoke?" she asked.

Wade closed the balcony doors and sniffed. "Yes, but it's coming from inside the hotel. There's a fire."

Theia turned toward the hotel door. "I've got to get back to my room and get my documents. I have letters from my grandmother and grandfather, photos, and other papers. They're priceless."

Wade pulled her back. "You're not going anywhere until we're given the all-clear."

"But my papers will burn up if I don't get them," Theia insisted.

"Would you rather burn up or rescue your papers?"

Theia cringed and turned around. "We could be burned alive, or we'll have to jump. We're on the fifth floor. We'll never make it."

"If there's a fire on our floor, we can sit in the bathtub and place some wet towels in the door opening until we're rescued. I saw that somewhere in a movie."

"We're going to die, aren't we?" Theia paced the room, agitated, limping as she walked, trying not to hyperventilate. Where was a paper bag when you needed one? Even if she had one she didn't know if she'd breathe into it or barf in it.

"No, we're not," Wade assured, voicing a certainty he didn't feel. "This is a big hotel. I'm sure the authorities will have this situation under control. It's just taking them time to get to us."

"How can you be so sure?"

"Because I didn't come all the way over here on my honeymoon to die in Florence, Italy."

"Your honeymoon? You're married? Where's your wife?"

"She didn't come. This was supposed to be our

honeymoon trip, but she backed out of the wedding at the last minute, so I came alone. The trip was already paid for. I think that's why the tour director thought you were my wife. All the reservations were for two."

"Is that why you rated this fancy suite?"

"It's the honeymoon suite. I'm glad I had someone to share it with."

"How long were you engaged?"

"About seven years."

"Seven years!"

"Well, we were dating for seven years before I asked her to marry me."

Theia tried to hold back her laughter. "Seven years? No wonder she dumped you. She probably got tired of waiting. I don't blame her."

"Marriage is for life. I had to be sure."

"Did you have to calculate the odds? Love doesn't work that way. Haven't you ever heard of love at first sight? Are all actuaries that cautious?"

"It's a casualty of the job."

"You bring the concept of cautious to a whole new level. While I, on the other hand, throw caution to the wind and jump into bed with total strangers."

"I'm hardly a stranger. I'm Wade…and don't you dare start singing. And you didn't jump into bed with me. You hobbled. What about you? Have you ever been in love?"

Theia hesitated. "Well, no."

"Why did you come on this trip?"

"I've always wanted to go to Italy. I'm a painter. All painters should go to Italy and study the great masters. My ya-ya gave me this trip before she died."

"Your ya-ya?"

"My grandmother. Also, my family has a history in Greece. After the tour, I'm going to make a pilgrimage to Crete, where my grandparents came from."

"Crete? You mean the home of the Minotaur, that monster with a human body and a bull's head that lived in the labyrinth? The creature that could only be satisfied with regular sacrifices of seven young men and seven maidens? The beast that was slain by Theseus?"

"I'm impressed. You know your Greek mythology."

"I have a photographic memory," Wade quipped.

"The Palace of Knossos is Crete's must-see historical attraction," said Theia.

"Right now, I'm not concerned about sightseeing. This situation is too unpredictable. Me, I want to get home as soon as possible," Wade said.

"*If* we make it out of here, you mean."

"*When* we make it out of here."

Another explosion rocked the hotel. It seemed to come from a lower floor. Theia jumped into Wade's arms, and he held her. "They're just hand grenades," Wade said. "It means the good guys are fighting back. Everything is going to be okay."

"Are you always so sure of yourself?"

"I'm only about eighty percent sure."

"I don't like those odds."

A few minutes passed. Theia's breath came in uneven spurts. "Wade, I'm terrified."

"So am I, but we'll be okay as long as we stay locked in our room."

"If they find me, they're going to kill me," Theia whispered against Wade's chest.

"Why?"

"Because I'm Jewish. I didn't wear my Jewish star necklace. I feel ashamed that I didn't bring it. It belonged to my grandmother, but my mother warned me against wearing it, and she's right. I know it isn't safe to be a Jew in Europe—or anywhere, really."

Wade kissed her lightly on the top of her head. "It won't come to that. These extremists are equal opportunity killers. They hate everyone: Americans, Christians, and Jews."

"Especially Jews. But Europe has been anti-Semitic over the ages. I just thought things were different in Italy—the cradle of the Renaissance, and all that." She paused and emitted a nervous laugh. "Just when you thought it was safe to go back into the water."

"I remember the time I did some consulting in Argentina."

"That's where many of the SS officers went after the war, to escape," Theia noted suspiciously.

"Right. So I met a lot of Germans who said they fought on the Eastern Front against the Russians during the war. Apparently the only Germans who fought on the Western Front were three old grandmothers with pitchforks."

"You're just making that up to keep my mind off what's happening."

"No, no, it's true."

"You can't really understand unless you're Jewish."

"You may be right."

"Even if the police knock on the door, I'm not coming out until I'm sure who it is."

"I think that's a wise course of action."

Wade walked Theia over to the bed. "You're shaking. And your face is pale. Sit down for a while. Try to relax. I'll get you a soda and some candy from the mini-bar, to keep up your strength."

"T-Thanks."

Wade grabbed two bottles of soda and some snacks and brought them over to the bedside table. "There's an electric kettle with a selection of teas and infusions, and a Nespresso coffeemaker."

Then he picked up the binder with information about the Palazzo Dei Fiori.

"I'm going to get familiar with the layout of the hotel, in case we need to escape," said Wade. "It says here we're only a block from the Florence Cathedral, the Piazza Signoria, the Uffizi Gallery, and the Ponte Vecchio. And they have a private observation deck overlooking the Florence Cathedral, with a 360-degree view of Florence."

"Right. What they fail to mention are the terrorists who are probably up there right now, scoping out the place."

Wade frowned in concentration while he studied an architectural sketch of the hotel. A few minutes later, he smiled.

"Theia, look at this." He pointed to a drawing in the notebook. "We're here, in the honeymoon suite. Now look at this schematic here that highlights the fire exits. Our suite is unique in that it's a corner unit and faces both the cathedral and a back street. There's a fire escape, a physical ladder leading from the balcony of the second window in the living room onto the street, here."

Theia rubbed her neck. "Are you proposing that we

walk out onto the fire escape and five stories down to the street?"

"Yes, exactly."

"But we'd be exposed to anyone, if we leave our room. You can see from the television that the outside of the hotel is all over the news. All eyes are on the hotel. If we climb down, we'd be sitting ducks for the terrorists on the street."

"No, but don't you see, the TV cameras are focused on the cathedral side. That's the best backdrop for all the stations. The cathedral says Florence. Nobody is looking at this small side street here behind the Florence Duomo. And besides, the fire escape is covered. It lets out behind this alcove, so no one will see us climbing down."

"What's the name of the street at the bottom?"

Wade frowned. "Piazza Delle Bullets."

"You're making that up."

"No, that's really the name of the street."

"That's a bad omen. And it's taking a big risk," Theia pointed out.

"That's what I get paid for, to calculate risk, and I think we have an eighty-nine percent chance of getting to safety."

"That's pretty precise, but I'm not sure I like those odds, either."

"Well, the alternative is we wait here to be blown up or burned alive or shot. The terrorists know we're holed up in our rooms. All they have to do is come and get us. They can pick us off one by one whenever they please. I say we take matters into our own hands and take our chances. I doubt if anyone knows about this fire escape. It only exists in our suite."

Theia hesitated. "I'm not sure."

"I think it's the right move, but I won't go without you."

"I'm not staying here alone." Theia made up her mind. "What should we take?"

"You don't have to take anything, but I'm going to take my wallet with plenty of Euros, a passport, some bottled water, and snacks."

Theia gritted her teeth. "I can't go anywhere without my passport. And I need to pick up my grandmother's photographs and letters."

"You don't have a choice. Do you really want to walk down to your room?"

Theia bit her lip. "No."

"We'll get everything later, then."

"Wouldn't it be better to go in the middle of the night?"

"That actually makes a lot of sense. The odds would certainly be in our favor. Let's study the map and see where we'd end up and how we could get to a police station from there."

"But if we go out in the middle of the night, none of the shops will be open. We'll be wandering around Florence in the dark. And what if the Italian police mistake us for terrorists and shoot us?"

"That's true. It might be better if we go during the daylight so we can run into a shop or a restaurant and have them call for help. Can you speak Italian?"

Theia shrugged. "*Dov'è il bagno?*"

"What does that mean?"

"Where is the bathroom?"

"That will come in handy," Wade said flatly.

"I can also say 'Excuse me.' '*Scusa.*' "

"Perfect. If we run into a terrorist we can say, "Excuse me, but where is the bathroom?"

Theia bristled. "Well, what can you say in Italian?"

"Spaghetti."

She shook her head. "Well, Wade in the Water, lead the way."

Wade began gathering his wallet, his passport, his cell phone, a street map of the city, two bottles of water, and snacks into a pillowcase. He tied the top corners together and slung the makeshift bag over his shoulder.

"I'm going to go first," he said. "That way if they shoot at us, they'll get me and you can scamper back up the fire escape. I'll be right behind you when you're backing down, so don't be afraid."

"I'll be afraid, don't worry, but I don't see any other way out of here if we wait around. It's open season on Jews."

Wade opened the second window and climbed out onto the balcony. He looked down. "There's no activity here. I think we're good." He climbed onto the fire escape and started down. "Okay, follow me."

Theia hoisted herself over the ledge and started climbing down the fire escape. After a couple of feet, they were completely hidden from view. Theia looked down and saw Wade a few feet below her, looking up.

"Come on, you can do it. I'm right here." He touched her heel. He was worried about her ankle, but the swelling seemed to have been reduced overnight. She was circling down at a steady pace.

"What if they're waiting down there at the bottom with guns?"

"Most likely it will be the Italian police. It's going to be okay."

"If you say so. I'm counting on you. If you're wrong…"

"Then you can blame me."

"I will. You can count on that."

Wade climbed down several more stories until he was almost at ground level.

Theia moved faster. "Not so fast, wait for me."

"I'm right here. I'll catch you if you fall." Wade squeezed Theia's foot lightly but possessively. "Just one more story," he whispered. "You can make it. How's the ankle?"

"Still sore, but I just want to get out of here."

"We're almost home, sweetheart." He brushed his hand against the bottom of her foot and rubbed it.

Theia was close to weeping at that endearment. "I wish I were home."

"Come on, you're just a few steps away. You're a trooper."

Wade reached the bottom rung and guided Theia the rest of the way. When she reached the bottom, he pulled her into his arms and held on tight. "We made it."

"Well, how do we know what we'll find when we step out of this cylinder protector thing?"

"We're out of the hotel, aren't we?"

"Yes."

"Then trust me." He took her hand, and they peeked around the corner. "Come on, let's see what's out here." They walked out of the protective covering and looked across the street.

"There's our hotel, surrounded by Italian police and helicopters." He looked up. "Here's a restaurant, Sasso Di Dante Antico Ristorante."

He pulled them inside.

She walked up to a waiter. "*Scusa, ma,* we need help." And then she fainted into Wade's arms.

Patrons and waiters gathered around Theia and fanned her with their menus.

"*Signorina, signorina.*"

Wade tried to explain their predicament, but the waiter spoke only broken English. A tourist finally understood that they had been in the hostage siege, and someone called the police. A police officer on a motorcycle pulled up in front of the restaurant.

Wade told the policeman where they had come from, and he made a call. Soon the restaurant was surrounded by police. Wade showed the police the way up to the hotel on the fire escape. They made more phone calls on their police radios. They spoke in Italian, barking orders. From what Wade understood, the police were going to climb back up into the honeymoon suite and storm the hotel from there. Within minutes a team of police with guns were headed toward the roof.

Theia swam back into consciousness.

"Give her some space," Wade said, indicating for the spectators to stand back. "She needs something to drink. A soda? Anything? We haven't eaten since yesterday."

"Ah," said the waiter. Food was a concept he understood. Within minutes, a platter of cheese, antipasto, and salad, with some fresh bruschetta, napkins, two plates, and silverware appeared before them. Then the waiter brought over drinks and two slices of pepperoni pizza.

Theia took a swig of the soda and stuffed the pizza into her mouth. "Mmm," she said, wolfing down the rest of the slice. She stabbed a slice of provolone with her fork and piled some salad on her plate.

"Wade, try this. It's amazing."

Wade followed suit. Suddenly, they heard rapid gunfire, followed by explosions that rocked the front of the Duomo for the next hour. They looked over at the hotel, and the windows were filled with smoke. People were running out of the front of the hotel, while police headed inside. The injured were carried out in stretchers. Some people were being brought down the fire escape and into the restaurant, which had become a staging area.

"What's going on?" Wade asked the restaurant owner.

"You are heroes. The police went up the fire escape and rescued the hostages on your floor and the other floors and brought them down, and then they went in after the terrorists. The siege is over."

"How many were hurt?"

The owner pointed to the copy scrolling across the bottom of the television. "All of the terrorists are dead, five hostages killed."

The police officers shook Wade and Theia's hands.

"Can we go back into the hotel and get our things?"

"Once we put out the fires," the policeman explained.

Theia breathed a sigh of relief. Wade called his parents. Theia called hers and assured them she was all right.

The tour guide came over to the restaurant to see Wade and Theia.

"Ah, the newlywed heroes. I heard what you did.

You took a big chance climbing down the building. But I'm glad you did."

"We're not newlyweds," Theia pointed out, but no one was listening. "When can we get back into our rooms?"

"In a few hours. Once we get everything settled, we'll continue with the tour."

Theia shook her head vehemently. "I-I'm leaving the tour."

"That is not necessary. But of course, that is your choice. You will get a full refund."

"I need to get to Greece, to Crete, to be exact." Theia asked the guide, "How do I do that?"

"Crete lies off Greece's southern coastline," said the guide. "You can go through Brindisi and take a ferry across, but that would take a long time. Or you could fly to Milan and then on to Crete. That would be the easiest route." He explained the options and agreed to make all the arrangements for them.

"So why exactly are you going to Crete?" asked Wade. "Why not Athens or Mykonos or Santorini? Those are the more popular tourist destinations."

"Because my grandmother was born in Crete, in Chania, and so was my real grandfather. He was a wonderful painter. I never met him. I didn't even know he existed until I read my grandmother's letters. Neither did my mother. I had planned to spend more time in Florence, studying the art at the galleries and in the churches."

"At least you got to see the Uffizi."

"It wasn't nearly enough time."

"I saw you crying in front of *The Birth of Venus*."

"Were you following me on every excursion?"

"You caught my attention from that first night at the reception," Wade admitted. "I wanted to meet you. I guess I have been following you. I almost came up to you in the museum then, but you looked like you wanted to be alone."

"I love Botticelli. If only I could paint like him."

"Are you a good artist?"

"I don't know how good I am, but I am an artist, like my grandfather."

"Would I have seen anything he painted?"

"No, he didn't survive the war. He was killed in a boat explosion on his way to Auschwitz. He didn't have a chance to make a name for himself. My grandfather was good enough to study under Chagall. He could have been the next Chagall or Monet. I often wonder what could have become of all those other lost souls. What they could have been, what they could have contributed to the world—to medicine, science, the arts, the love they could have found, the children they could have had. Think about the six million people who perished in the Holocaust, their potential, what the world lost.

"I would have loved to see my grandfather's work," Theia continued. "It could have been an inspiration. But I paint because I have to. People say it's a gift. I have to be true to it. I dream about my paintings before I paint them. I see scenes in my head. I wonder if my grandfather did the same thing. There is one scene I keep seeing over and over, but it's too terrible to put on canvas. I've been dreaming about it ever since I found out what happened to my grandfather."

"What scene is that?"

"The night my grandfather died. The same night my mother was born."

Wade opened his mouth to speak, but Theia put her finger to his lips to quiet him. "Do you believe in heaven?"

"I don't think much about it."

"I do. I was with my grandmother the night she died, and she reached out her hand to someone and smiled. She was the happiest I'd ever seen her. I saw a young man, very handsome, standing at the foot of the bed. I didn't know who he was until I found the photographs. But I know she saw my grandfather. He was looking as young as he was the day he died."

"What photographs?"

"I didn't find them until my grandmother died and we cleaned out her house. They were in a shoebox in her closet. There were the pictures of my grandmother and the grandfather I never knew and their families. And their letters, his to her and hers to him. That's when I found the letter asking me to go back, to add our pictures to the wall of photos in the synagogue to show that our family had survived. All of the other families, except ours, had already returned, made their pilgrimage to the synagogue to post pictures of their families. When I read the letters, saw the pictures, I knew I had to come. My grandmother had already given me a gift of this tour when I graduated college. So I thought I'd take a tour of Italy and make my way to Crete afterward. I'm glad we had a few days in Florence before the attack. Didn't you love the Uffizi Gallery? I could have spent all day there. And there is wonderful art everywhere in this city, everywhere you turn, especially in the churches."

"Is that one of the reasons you're going to Greece? For the art?"

"Of course I'm interested in the art, but it's mostly to find out more about my heritage. My family roots are in Greece, so I'm making a pilgrimage. And who knows what fate has in store for me? Maybe I'll meet my future husband. My grandmother always said she wanted me to marry a Greek man. Now I think I understand why. I'm hoping to find inspiration for my paintings. The views are supposed to be breathtaking, the beaches gorgeous, the blue of the water and the stunning simplicity of the white architecture a stark contrast, which I'm hoping to capture in my own work, or at least allow to influence it."

"You believe in fate?"

"Of course. I'm Greek."

"And I trust the odds," Wade said. "The odds of you falling in love when you get to Crete and meeting the man you are going to marry are not in your favor. And how do you know you haven't met him already?"

Theia shook her head. "Just keep those negative thoughts to yourself."

"Won't you be disappointed if we don't finish the tour?"

"I'd love to see Capri and Venice; of course I would. And my painter's education wouldn't be complete without a visit to Rome. Rome would have been the next stop on the tour, but I'm glad to be done with it. It's jinxed. I think I'll just go on my own and make my way over to Crete."

"Want some company?" Wade asked. "I've never seen Greece."

"I thought you wanted to go home."

Wade stared into Theia's eyes. "I'm not ready for this trip to end."

"Well, suit yourself. If you want to tag along, I wouldn't mind."

Wade grinned and took another bite of his pizza.

"How did you say your grandfather died?"

"It's a long, sad story. I'll tell you when we get to Crete."

Part Two
Theia's Journey

"A painting is not thought out in advance. While it is being done, it changes as one's thoughts change. And when it's finished, it goes on changing, according to the state of mind of whoever is looking at it."

~Pablo Picasso

Marilyn Baron

Chapter Three

Theia and Wade rested side by side on lounge chairs on the upper deck as the ferry sliced through the Ionian Sea toward the Mediterranean and Crete. Wade had concocted a makeshift arrangement of towels to elevate Theia's foot.

"How's your ankle?" he asked.

"Much better, thanks to you."

Theia's body was relaxed, calmed by the movement of the vessel and warmed by the sun. She was as loose as a lounge lizard. Wade was turning pea soup green on the shifting deck.

"Remind me why we didn't fly?"

"Because you wanted to save money," Theia said, smiling. "That's the actuary in you. I, on the other hand, was up for adventure, thus the ferry."

Theia rooted around in her beach bag and took out a handful of wrapped candies. "Here, take these."

"What are they?"

"Ginger candies."

"What will they do?"

"They'll keep you from puking all over me and the boat. Seriously, they should help with your motion sickness."

Wade accepted her offer, reaching out for the organic remedy. "Beware of Greeks bearing gifts," he said, popping a piece of the candy in his mouth and pocketing the rest.

"Ha, ha. How original. I've never heard that one before."

"Sorry," he said.

"Ginger doesn't work for everyone, but it's usually pretty effective. And focus on the horizon; don't look down."

Wade's eyes were fixed on hers.

"And don't look at me."

Wade lifted his eyes toward the sea. "You're right. We should have flown. I'll know better next time."

"Well, we're almost there. And I love being on the open water. To me, it's the only way to see a city when you travel."

"Well, I'm Swiss, so we're landlocked."

"Swiss? Is that what you are? How convenient. Mr. Neutrality, don't rock the boat, no pun intended."

"What is that supposed to mean?"

"Take it however you want," Theia retorted. "Are you sure you booked us a hotel on the island?"

"Of course. I'm nothing if not organized."

"I appreciate you floating me the money. We're not getting reimbursed for our tour for a few weeks, and I'm sort of short on cash. Artists don't make much, but I promise I'll pay you back."

"I'm happy to do it. Like I said, I've never been to Greece, and I've always wanted to go. I hear it's beautiful. And so is the present company."

Theia smiled demurely. "I've never been either, but the way my grandmother's letters describe it, it sounds like paradise. And after what we've been through, I think we deserve some relaxation."

"I couldn't agree more. And thanks for the ginger. I'm feeling a lot better."

Theia handed Wade a bottle of water and a pill. "Take this ginger pill now and another one tomorrow morning, and you should be fine. Your color is improving already." Theia's hand cradled Wade's cheek. He shivered at her touch.

"Are you cold?" she worried.

"No," he said simply. "Theia, can you speak Greek?"

"Of course. That's all my ya-ya spoke at home."

"Great, because when I looked at the newspaper on board, it was all Greek to me."

"You're a riot, Wade. How long have you been waiting to use that line?"

Wade smiled, and his eyes sparkled.

Theia studied him. She had to admit, this trip would not have been the same without him. She'd never tell Wade, but she was glad he had agreed to accompany her on this journey. He was a handy man to have around. He'd kept her calm during a crisis.

"Hey, Theia, I never asked. Do you have any brothers or sisters?"

"All brothers, except for me. I'm the youngest of six, so they're very protective of me. My parents adore each other. Pregnancy was my mother's natural state for quite a few years."

"Do you ever want to have children?"

"Of course. That's expected."

"But do *you* want them?"

"Yes, don't you?"

"Yes. That's one of the reasons we broke off our engagement. My fiancée didn't want children. She was more focused on her career."

"Do you miss her?"

Wade paused. "I thought I would. I mean, I would have missed her company, but I have you now. And I— thought I was in love with her, but—"

"But what?"

Wade fixed her with his eyes. "I didn't know what real love was."

Wade knew how to behave around women. His two sisters had taught him that much. He knew to compliment women on their clothes and their hair. In fact, he knew a lot about women's clothes, designers and styles. One of his sisters was a fashion consultant. He also knew enough to say, "No!" when a woman asked if she looked too fat in a particular outfit. But he'd never been tongue-tied around a woman like he was around Theia. He'd never been so turned around he couldn't think straight. And he'd never been so sure about how he felt about a woman in his whole life.

He needed to use every moment to his advantage before she set out on her quest to snag a Greek husband who was also Jewish, neither qualities he could claim. As farfetched as Theia's goals seemed, he was not going to let that happen. Theia was "the one" and he wasn't going to let her get away.

Chapter Four

Theia and Wade walked up the blue flagstone path in the courtyard approaching the entrance of the Etz Hayyim Synagogue. Her limp was hardly noticeable.

With the open palm of her hand, she touched the warm, whitewashed stone wall framed in ivy. "Isn't it beautiful? It's the only surviving, functioning synagogue on Crete. I read that it's been restored and that it was re-dedicated in October 1999. It has a *mikveh* and has become a tourist destination."

"What's a *mikveh*?" asked Wade.

"A Jewish ritual bath," answered Theia. "It's fed by a spring."

"I feel like a fish out of water here," he observed. "I'm not Greek and I'm not Jewish."

"That's silly. You'll be fine."

They crossed the threshold to the synagogue together, walking in out of the sun into a cool place that felt like home.

An elderly woman sat on a chair inside the sanctuary. As they entered, she struggled as she got up from her seat to approach Theia with tears in her eyes.

"Is it really you?"

"Do you know me?" Theia asked, puzzled.

"It's just that you look so much like her. Like someone I once knew many years ago. My childhood friend, Eleni. Or maybe I'm seeing a ghost."

"Eleni was my ya-ya, my grandmother."

"You must be Theia. Your mother called and said you'd be coming."

Theia nodded and turned to Wade. "And this is my friend, Wade."

The woman nodded to Wade but put her arms around Theia. "I'm Sophia. I've been waiting a long time for you."

"When my grandmother passed away, we found a shoebox full of pictures. My mother and I read through her letters, and she thought I should deliver the photographs in person. I'm from one of the six families whose children escaped from Chania during the war. I've come from America to post my family's pictures on the Memory Wall that I read about on the Internet."

"You look just so much like your grandmother, it's uncanny. And yet I see a lot of your grandfather in you, too. Your mother told me about Eleni's passing. I was sorry to hear that. I would have loved to have seen her one more time." Sophia continued to cry silent tears, then dried her eyes with the back of her gnarly hands as Theia reached out to comfort her. "Later, we'll post the pictures, but first let's sit and talk. Make yourselves comfortable."

Theia and Wade took seats next to each other, across from the woman.

"You knew my grandfather, too?"

"Yes, of course. We all grew up together."

"I want to hear all about him."

"And you will. But first let me tell you about our synagogue."

"The look of this place is different from our synagogue at home," said Theia, "but it feels familiar, although I've never been here before."

"That is a very common feeling," noted Sophia. "Everyone says that. The layout of the interior of our synagogues is more typical of synagogues in Venice, North Africa, and the western islands of Greece. The *bimah* and the *Sepher Torah* are on opposite sides of the sanctuary." She pointed out the locations. The ark faced the eastern wall, the *bimah* the western one.

Wade observed the arched doorways, the colorful Turkish carpets on the black and white tiles, the inlaid wooden ceiling, and the wooden benches. "The interior design looks Moroccan, sort of a Moorish motif," he observed.

"You have a good eye," said Sophia. "That's because we're Judeo-Spanish."

Theia turned to Wade. "Have you ever been in a synagogue before?"

"Well, no."

"The synagogue's layout is in the Romaniote tradition," Sophia said.

"That means Greek," Theia explained.

"Originally, there were two synagogues built in the Jewish quarter of Chania, Crete's second-largest city," said Sophia. "Etz Hayyim, here, and Beth Shalom, the synagogue used by the Sephardi Jews of Chania. That one was completely bombed into ruins in 1941. Etz Hayyim was abandoned when the Jewish community dissolved in 1944. Many years later, in the mid-1990s, our synagogue, the one that hadn't been destroyed during the bombardment, was restored. This is the only structure of Jewish significance on the island of Crete. It's also the only memorial to our last Jewish community.

"Very few Jewish people were lucky enough to escape the Nazis," explained Sophia. "By the end of the war, the Jewish community of Chania was virtually eliminated. Today, there are only a dozen Jews left in Crete. We hold weekly Shabbat services attended by tourists and synagogue friends from other cities, often non-Jews, and a rabbi comes from Athens or another island to help with Rosh Hashanah and Yom Kippur services. Occasionally, someone who can blow the shofar visits the community at the Jewish holidays. We're pretty crowded on Passover. Sometimes people hold weddings and bar mitzvahs here, since it's the island's only remaining synagogue.

"Almost all of the congregants are non-Jews," added Sophia. "We don't often have services. We don't even have enough congregants to hold a *minyan*. An international team takes care of the congregation work."

"I'm sorry to sound so ignorant, but what's a *minyan*?" Wade asked.

"The number of men—a quorum of ten—required for Jewish communal worship," Theia explained. She turned to Sophia. "How long have you been here?"

"Since the war," Sophia said.

"How did you—?"

"Survive the war? A few of the families, and children, like me, evaded the roundup right before the deportation. I was taken in and hidden by a Greek Orthodox family. And after the synagogue was restored, I've been here waiting. I gathered all the photographs I had saved from the streets after the roundup and mounted them on a remembrance wall in our little museum. I believe I was spared for a purpose, to be the keeper of those memories. I have many beautiful memories of your grandmother and grandfather in my heart. I still miss her. We were as close as sisters."

"I was in the room with her when she took her last breath," said Theia. "I was relieving my mother, who rarely left her side at the end. But I think she waited until my mother was out of the room for permission to go. At the end of the bed there was a man, a young man, very handsome. She reached out to him and she smiled. She was the happiest I've seen her in a long time—well, ever, really."

"You saw this young man?"

"Yes," said Theia. "As plain as you're sitting here now."

Sophia looked through the photographs in Theia's envelope and pulled out a picture.

"Did he look like this?"

"Yes."

"That was Theo, her husband. You were obviously named for him. Theo and Eleni grew up in Chania, played together as children, and fell in love. I've never seen a happier couple or two people more in love. From the moment they met, there was no one else for the other. He was her life and she was his. Everyone knew they would get married. It was a tragedy that they could not spend their lives together. That's what war does. Luckily, your grandmother was spared the horrors of the destruction of our community in 1944. Although she wasn't so lucky because she lost the love of her life."

"I read the letters, but I'd like to hear the story from you. Maybe you could fill in some of the blanks."

Sophia sighed. "Of course. But first, let me finish showing you and your friend around our little synagogue, and then we'll see the wall of life."

Sophia tottered in front of them, leading the way.

"Our present *Sepher*, written on gazelle skin and housed in a fine olive *tik*, or wooden case, was provided by the London Scrolls Trust.

"These nineteen benches were made in Jakarta," continued Sophia, gesturing to the middle of the sanctuary. "Our Torahs were some of the 1,574 Torahs discovered in an abandoned synagogue near Prague in 1945 and restored to Jewish communities. They had all been stolen from synagogues in Eastern Europe."

Theia picked up a prayer book.

"Services, when we have them, are conducted in Hebrew, Greek, and English, so our prayer books are in English, Greek, and Hebrew," Sophia explained.

Theia smiled. She could read from any one of them with ease, and she also spoke Ladino, the form of Judeo-Spanish her ya-ya had often spoken at home.

Wade picked up the Greek version of the prayer book and glanced at Theia with an impish smile.

"Don't even think about opening your smart mouth," Theia warned in a whisper.

"What?" Wade asked innocently throwing up his hands in mock affront, barely concealing a lopsided grin. "You don't even know what I was going to say."

"Oh, but I do. You were going to say, 'It's all Greek to me,' weren't you?"

Wade colored and placed the prayer book sheepishly back in its holder.

"Turns out all the women in your life were wrong. You do have a sense of humor. It's just a bad one. This is a house of worship. Please try to act accordingly."

Wade drew a deep breath at Theia's verbal lashing. "Be careful, your bossy side is showing."

"I'm not bossy." Theia frowned, punched his arm, and turned away.

"Sorry," Wade whispered, taking Theia's hand and squeezing it.

Sophia flashed a knowing smile at the sparring couple and proudly showed them around the research library. "I'm just a volunteer. We're completely self-supporting. In 2010, we had two arsons in one month, which almost destroyed the library and office. We think the motive was anti-Semitism or robbery or both. But thanks to international donations, we were able to make repairs. Since there aren't many permanent resident Jewish families, we continue to depend on benefactors and visitor donations."

"Imagine, Wade. This synagogue has been around since the Middle Ages." Theia indicated a Tzedakah bowl, and Wade deposited some currency into it.

"This is like passing the plate in church," he whispered.

Theia nodded.

They moved into an anteroom. On the far wall was a kaleidoscope of pictures—of small children laughing and playing, newborns, newlyweds dressed in their wedding finery and starting their lives together, Bar and Bat Mitzvah ceremonies, portraits of families dressed for the holidays.

"The story I tell everyone who visits the synagogue is that Theo, your grandfather, had the foresight to arrange for a Jewish organization to place five children, along with your grandmother who was pregnant at the time with their child, in Jewish homes away from Crete. It saved their lives and preserved our congregation. Specifically, six of our children were saved—including your mother—and taken in by families across the world. One of our children went to South Africa, one to Argentina, one to Los Angeles, one to Australia, and two, including your mother, with your grandmother, to Atlanta. Did the two Atlanta families ever get together?"

"Yes," Theia said. "My grandmother was offered a room in the house of a very generous congregant who had agreed to raise one of the boys who traveled with her. After my mother was born, she and my grandmother continued to live in that house because they had nowhere else to go. My grandmother eventually married the head of the household, after his wife passed away, and the two children, my mother and the boy who came with my grandmother, fell in love and married each other."

"How wonderful. That's *bashert*. So your grandmother and your mother preserved our heritage. It must have been a great cause for celebration."

"Well, I wasn't around, of course, but I'm here now."

"So those are the descendants of the six. Our congregation is not lost." She pointed to the wall. "You see, I receive photos from families from all over the world so people will know that we survived."

Theia ceremoniously presented the envelope of pictures she had carried all the way from the United States to Sophia. The synagogue caretaker reopened the envelope. Tears flowed from her eyes again, and she hugged Theia tightly. "You do resemble your grandfather. Look, here, you have the same space between your teeth. And you have his eyes."

Theia studied the picture of her grandfather and blushed. It must be hereditary. She pushed her tongue up and rubbed it against the space. She'd grown up hating that space, but her grandfather had the same space between his teeth, so they shared that and their passion for art. That was a comforting thought. And she was the only one in her family with green eyes, like her grandfather's.

"You help me hang the photographs," Sophia suggested.

"I'd like that."

She and Sophia worked silently to hang the pictures of her ya-ya, her real grandfather, her mother and father, and herself with her brothers. Then, of course, there were the aunts and uncles, her mother's siblings, born to her grandmother and step-grandfather.

"You have a beautiful family," said the woman. "A big family."

"Almost big enough to repopulate Chania," Theia answered.

"You are the descendants of Theo and Eleni Frangos. You can be very proud. And one day you will have your own Greek family."

Theia blushed, and Wade frowned.

"I wish I had known him. He was a painter, like me. Have you seen his work?"

"Oh, Theo was a brilliant artist," said Sophia. "Had he lived, there is no doubt he would have been one of the greats. You know he studied with Chagall in

France?"

"I read about that in my grandmother's letters. Until then, I had no idea who he was, or even that he was an artist."

"Oh, yes. He was a genius. Everybody thought so. The world has rarely seen a talent such as his. If he hadn't been taken so young—" The woman paused for emphasis. "*Killed.* There is no telling what he could have become. His work was uplifting. It captured the beauty in the world. That was the unique way he saw things."

"My grandmother never talked about him. Not even to my mother. I never saw a picture of him or heard about him. It was only after she died and we found her letters that we saw pictures of them together in Chania. I didn't even know she had been married to someone before Papou. I've never seen his paintings."

"They were, in a word, marvelous. They were all lost in a fire during a bombing in the war."

"That's a shame. Now I shall never see them. I don't know if I paint like him or if our styles are at all similar."

"So you want to be an artist like your grandfather?"

"Yes."

"Your parents must be proud of you."

"Proud, yes, but they have expectations," Theia said. "My ya-ya wanted me to marry a Greek man, a Jewish man, and have many children, just like my mother did."

"A noble aspiration, certainly," said Sophia.

Wade folded his arms defiantly across his chest.

"They care more about that, I think, than my aspirations as a painter. The artistic gene skipped a generation. My mother was definitely not a painter. Her children were her works of art."

"It's amazing how much you look like them," Sophia repeated, pointing on the wall to the wedding portrait of Theia's grandparents.

"I wonder why my grandmother never talked about her life on Crete," Theia said. "It must have been too painful that their life together was cut so short."

"But they had your mother, and then your mother had you," the woman said.

"But how sad is that. They were so in love, and my grandfather never even saw his child."

"How much do you know about your grandfather?" Sophia asked.

"Only that he was an artist."

"He was so talented that Marc Chagall took an interest in his career, as I mentioned. He went to France to study with the great master for a year. Your grandmother was so in love with him that she wanted what was best for him, and so she let him go. Your grandfather's style was very similar to the great master's—light, whimsical, dreamy. Your grandfather drew pictures of Chania, of the people, the scenery, especially the beaches, and many of your grandmother. He always said his pictures came alive from his dreams."

"I also dream and then paint what's in my dreams," said Theia. "I dreamed of this place before I knew anything about it."

"Perhaps you have your grandfather's spirit within you."

"What happened to my grandfather? I know my grandmother received word of a tragedy at sea. He was supposed to meet her in Atlanta, but he never came. She alluded to his death in one of her letters, the last one she wrote to him, but if you don't mind, I'd like to hear the story about what happened in Chania during the war."

"That's why I'm here. I come every day for the tourists, to tell them about the Jews of Chania, so no one will forget and no one can claim it never happened. You've heard of the Holocaust deniers?"

"Yes," said Theia. She looked intently at Wade, daring him to speak.

"I'm not a denier," Wade protested, holding up his hand. "It's true I don't know anything about the Nazi occupation of Greece. The truth is that the amount I know about the Holocaust could fit into a thimble. I haven't really thought much about it. But looking at those pictures, especially the wedding photo of your grandparents, looking at each other like they were the only two people in the world, breaks my heart. Theia, you are the incarnation of your grandmother. But for a brief lapse in time, that could have been you who…"

Theia nodded. She had been thinking the same thing. "I only know what I have read. My grandmother never told me anything, so what I know about her life is only from her letters. I'm hoping we can find out some history inside this building."

"Let's start from the beginning," said Sophia. "You have to do that to understand what was happening in Europe at the time. In 1937, about twenty thousand works from German museums, including Chagall's, were confiscated as "degenerate." Marc Chagall was living in Vichy, France, and he was so preoccupied with his art he wasn't aware until October 1940 of the danger French Jews faced. He almost didn't get out. He was a prominent artist, so naturally he thought his fame would protect him. Maybe he thought the rules didn't apply to him.

"France collapsed so quickly everyone was caught unprepared. Jews were being rounded up and sent to concentration camps. Nazi occupying forces began approving anti-Semitic laws, and Jews were being removed from public and academic positions. But stubbornly he failed to see the predicament he was in and the position he put his family in. But as he witnessed the growing violence and persecution of the Jews, he realized he had to leave France to save his family, and he sought to emigrate to America. Jews in Germany often waited years for permission to emigrate.

"As I said, Theo had gone to France to study with Chagall. It was a once-in-a-lifetime opportunity. Eleni didn't go with him, but she didn't want him to pass up this chance. Your grandfather was there in Vichy, France, with Chagall and his family when war broke out. With the help of the director of the Museum of Modern Art, an American journalist, the American Vice-Consul in Marseilles, and the Emergency Committee to Save European Jewry, who smuggled European artists and intellectuals out of Europe and to the United States under forged visas, Marc Chagall and his family escaped to the USA and took with them his paintings and Theo's paintings—the ones he'd created in France.

"Chagall and his wife, Bella, fled to New York City and arrived on June 23, 1941, the day after Germany invaded the Soviet Union and the same year Crete was taken by the Germans. He was one of 2,000 who were rescued by this operation. Chagall's daughter

Ida and her husband Michel followed on the refugee ship *SS Navemar* with a large case of Chagall's and Theo's work. Picasso and Matisse were also among artists invited to America, but they decided to stay in France.

"They offered to help your grandfather make arrangements for passage for himself and your grandmother, but at that time the war had not yet come to Crete, and she refused to leave her parents. Most of us felt the same. We thought we were untouchable, that nothing bad could happen to us. We were wrong. Of course your grandfather wouldn't go without Eleni. They lived happily together for a short while, until the Germans came to Crete, and then your grandfather joined the forces fighting for Greece in the mountains. He felt it was his duty. But he tried to convince us. He returned from France talking of trouble for the Jews there. But no one listened."

"How long were my grandparents reunited before my grandfather enlisted? Did he ever return for her?"

"For only a brief while. That was a tragic story."

"Can you tell me more?" Theia prompted.

"I will tell you what I know," said Sophia, who settled down across from them on the bench in front of the memory wall. "The war in Crete began in 1941 and lasted until 1945. For two weeks in May of 1941, three of our main towns were badly bombed by the German Luftwaffe, commanded by General Wolfram Freiherr von Richthofen, of the Condor Legion."

"Wasn't that the same Condor Legion of Hitler's German air force that destroyed the village of Guernica, Spain, on April 26, 1937?" Wade interjected.

"Wade has a photographic memory where he stores

a warehouse full of useless facts," Theia said.

"He's right, and it's a very relevant fact," said Sophia. "That was the first-ever aerial bombardment of a civilian population, and it destroyed seventy percent of the village, killing and wounding about 1,600 people, roughly one-third of the population of Guernica. Perhaps you've heard about Picasso's painting, *Guernica*, that showed the results of bombing."

"Of course," said Theia. "I've studied that painting. It's one of my favorites."

"Because of its elongated shape and mountainous terrain, the island of Crete was ideal for the establishment of local guerilla groups and resistance fighters. From the moment the German offensive began, and over the years of occupation that followed, civilians set up armed groups to defend the island. Then came the waves of paratroopers. When the Germans took Crete, they were met by fierce resistance from the local population. In addition to other activities, we gave shelter to British Commonwealth soldiers and assisted them in escaping.

"Crete's three main towns—Chania, Rethmynon, and Heraklion—were badly bombed. The worst bombing was right here in Chania. By June of 1941, the Axis Powers had won the Battle of Crete. The island was divided into two occupation zones. The Germans took the main ports and cities, and the Italians held the far eastern portion."

At this point in her story, Sophia's eyes became glassy and her voice seemed far away, as if she were slipping back in time.

Chapter Five

*Crete during the German-Italian Occupation,
1941-1944*

"Look what they've done, Eleni! They've destroyed my studio! Everything is gone! A lifetime of work, blown to dust in seconds."

Eleni gently cradled Theo's cheek with the palm of her hand to calm him. "Darling, didn't you say the paintings you created in France are on a boat to New York? Your work will be preserved."

Despondent, Theo flung Eleni's hand from his face. "The work I did in France, yes. But not my work in Chania. It's ruined, everything is ruined." His voice stung like a slap in the face.

"Theo, we still have each other."

"Eleni, how many times have I warned you we've got to get away from here? I've seen the war in France. I've seen the cruelty of the Germans. I've told you it was only a matter of time, and now they're here. You're blind if you can't see that."

Sophia arrived at what was left of Theo's studio.

"My God, Theo! Your beautiful paintings! They're gone!"

"I wish you would explain to your friend, the ostrich here, who won't take her beautiful head out of the sand, that we cannot stay here a moment longer."

Eleni embraced Sophia. "You're all right?"

"I'm fine, but our city is all but destroyed. Theo's right, Eleni. I've been taken in by a Greek Orthodox family. I'm safe. But Theo is a partisan known to the Germans. You are his wife. If they catch him, they will execute him as an example. You've got to leave now."

"How safe do you think you'll be if the Germans find out you're with the resistance too, my friend?"

Sophia raised her head in defiance. "That's a chance I'll have to take."

"It's all bluster," said Eleni, waving her hands in front of her face. "They've dropped their bombs and split up our country between them, and now what else can they do? We'll wait it out until it blows over."

"Blows over?" Theo raged. "Do you hear yourself, Eleni? It is not a mistral that blows in and out again. It's not a game. You think things cannot get worse, but I assure you they can."

"But the Allies—" Eleni protested.

"Have pulled back and already begun their evacuation to Egypt," Theo interrupted. "The Fifth Cretan Division retreated to the Peloponnese and they've all but dissolved. There's no way for it to reach Crete."

"What about the three battalions that remained in Crete after the rest of the division was transferred to the mainland?"

"They participated in the Battle of Crete, and we know how that turned out."

"But surely someone—"

"There's no one left to defend us. No one left but our people to resist."

"We're like the unsuspecting lobsters in a pot of

warm water," sighed Sophia. "We're comfortable, but they will turn up the heat, and then we will boil to death, slowly, and we won't even know what happened. Theo, I came to tell you. The German High Command asked the rabbi of Chania for an initial list of the Jewish community and its members."

"That's how it starts," Theo ranted. "That's exactly how it starts. Next there will be a series of anti-Jewish measures imposed. Jewish newspapers will close down. Jewish families will be forced to wear the Star of David and kicked out of their homes and arrested. And despite these warnings, you're reluctant to leave your home? Before you know it, the *Wehrmacht* will begin hunting down and executing innocent civilians around the island for acts of resistance."

"They've already begun executing and imprisoning civilians for resisting German occupation," attested Sophia. "No one is safe, Christians or Jews. They're massacring everyone, including lawyers and teachers, farmers and politicians, even journalists and a priest. Our cities, towns, and villages are destroyed, deserted."

Theo chimed in. "I've just heard about some soldiers who surrounded a local village, gathered the people together in the main square, and began interrogating them. They beat them. Then they arbitrarily selected the people they wanted to execute and did it, without a care. They're looting our houses, taking food and jewelry. They've even taken our sheep and goats. Whatever they can't take away, they destroy, then blow up the houses or burn them down."

"Surely they wouldn't do that," said Eleni.

Theo's face was enraged with frustration. "You are a child, Eleni, a blind child! I want to shake you. Wake up and look around you before it's too late."

Eleni shrank back. She hardly recognized Theo. He had changed since coming back from France.

Sophia put her hand on Theo's shoulder. "Please, do not take this out on Eleni. None of this is her fault."

"I had a way out for us and she refused to take it. She wouldn't leave, and I won't leave without her. To make matters worse, she's pregnant."

"To make matters worse?" Eleni questioned.

"You know what I mean. You need to get out. I need you and our child safe."

Sophia shook her head. "I tried to convince her to go. Dozens of families are homeless, Theo. Their military just comes in and destroys our homes or commandeers the homes they want. There are already food and medicine shortages. People are hungry and afraid. Pretty soon they'll devalue our money. The prices of olive oil, wheat, and leather are out of control. It is almost impossible to come by coffee and sugar."

"The black markets will take care of that," Theo spat.

"We've lost our freedom. The mountains, harbors, and beaches are 'off limits,' and they've imposed a curfew. They've cut off electrical power and confiscated our boats, and our vehicles and horses and hunting guns and radios. They loot our shops and take what they want. What's next?"

"They're already requisitioning our farmland and clear-felling our forests," Theo added.

"They're conscripting people of all ages for forced labor on road construction and building projects, and feeding them on starvation rations."

"But if they need us for work, surely they will keep

us around," Eleni reasoned.

"Eleni, don't you see? That's how it starts with occupying forces. They are killing Jews in Europe, taking them away for work and then eradicating them."

"But not here in Greece."

"Not now, but soon."

"But Theo, I'm pregnant. Surely they wouldn't harm a pregnant woman."

Fear was written all over Theo's face. "You are so naïve, Eleni. It's people like you who make their job easy. You go along like sheep to the slaughter. My God, what am I going to do with you? How can we bring a child into this world? Are we insane?"

Eleni rubbed her stomach. "Don't you want this child, Theo?"

Theo grabbed his bride and nearly crushed her in his arms. "Eleni, my love, there's nothing I want more than to have a nice, peaceful life with you and our child. But that is not up to us anymore. I love you more than life itself, and now you will do what I say. There's a boat, there's one more boat, and I want you to be on it."

"And you will come with me?"

"Eleni, what kind of a man would I be if I deserted my people when they need me? This country needs every man and woman it can get. Civilian heroes are risking their lives every day, heroes like your friend Sophia. I must do my part and stay and fight. I promise you I will be on the first boat out after the war is over. I will find you. But you have to promise me to protect our child—and the other children we're sending with you. Sophia, you take Eleni to the boat and make sure she and the children get away. I need to disappear back into the hills."

He held Sophia's chin with his fingers. "And dear Sophia, please take care. You are engaged in dangerous business."

"No more than you, my friend."

Theo turned to Eleni. "Sweetheart, I am sorry I lost my temper. I'll love you with my last breath." Theo kissed Eleni's tearstained face and held her like he would never see her again. She clung to him like a survivor to a life raft. He memorized her face and touched her lips with his fingertips. He remembered happier days when he had the luxury of time to paint her likeness. But they had run out of time. He placed his hand firmly on her stomach. "Take care of your mother, little one. I'll see you both again, in a better world."

Theo broke away with tears in his eyes and watched Eleni and Sophia as they walked toward the sea.

Chapter Six

Present Day Crete

"Did they ever see each other again after that?" Theia asked, dabbing her eyes.

"Not in this life," said Sophia, misty-eyed herself. "The Germans picked him up soon after that. He was caught up in the roundup. If he had stayed in the hills, he might still be alive. But he had to see Eleni one more time, to make sure she was safely away. I was a little bit in love with Theo too," she admitted. "It was hard not to be. His loss was my loss, too. But he only had eyes for Eleni."

Theia had listened intently and patiently, but she could no longer wait to hear about the *Tanais* tragedy. "What about the ship? Tell me more about what happened to the Jews of Chania, in particular to my grandfather."

"There have been Jews on Crete for about twenty-three hundred years," Sophia said. "And in fifteen minutes Cretan Jewish history was obliterated. We were just a tiny, mountainous island in the middle of the Mediterranean. We didn't have much—some buildings, shops, schools, synagogues, cemeteries. Only about twenty-five Jews from Crete survived the war.

"Before things got worse, your grandfather arranged for a man to take your grandmother and five children to Palestine and on to their journeys around the world, but at first she refused to go. She wouldn't leave your grandfather. Theo was not in Chania when the Germans began their roundups. He was in the mountains with the other partisans. When I got word to him that Eleni wouldn't leave without him, he snuck back, which was very dangerous, and convinced her to go on the very last ship, to protect their child and five other children. He risked his life to make sure for himself that she was on that boat. She wanted to wait for him, but in the end, the ship was ready to leave, the Germans came, and she had no choice. She had to protect her unborn child and the others in her care. He promised he would follow soon after.

"It was a heartbreaking and tearful last goodbye. A very pregnant Eleni clung to Theo. She and her charges of five Jewish refugee children, of all different grade school ages, were dressed for the weather—hats and headscarves, woolen stockings, heavy coats, and sturdy shoes or boots. All carried rolled sleeping bags, and duffel bags or knapsacks full of warm things for the journey and their life ahead. They wore several layers of clothing under their coats, with diamonds and paper money sewn into the hems of their jackets. The girls had purses stuffed with various little things. All had identifying tags on their belongings, and they clutched their all-important papers.

"A Jewish organization with the help of worldwide benefactors offered support in the rescue effort of the children of Chania. The Jewish Agency of Palestine, in Jerusalem, arranged for the dangerous transfer and 'illegal' emigration of unaccompanied Jewish children from Greece to Palestine and on to destinations around the world. Their parents had made the ultimate sacrifice to let them go, because otherwise they would see their children face deportation and almost certain death. Eleni was the adult chosen to accompany them as they were smuggled to safety. The *Yishuv*—the Jewish settlement in Palestine—organized this dangerous rescue of children from Crete to Palestine on Aliyah Bet ships from Greek ports, and Eleni left under cover of darkness on one of the last of the Aliyah Bet ships. Her group was lucky. They didn't drown on the difficult voyage.

"It was not until the morning hours of May 29th, 1944, that the Jews in the Old City of Chania were arrested in the Jewish quarter without warning. People were uprooted from their homes, their schools, their workplaces, stores, and their friends and marched out of their neighborhoods and down to the harbor by soldiers. They lost everything they had worked for all their lives, had to leave everything behind, even their photographs. They were herded together and transferred into a convoy of trucks, taken to Ayias Prison, located not far from Chania. When I got back from the docks, your grandfather had been caught in the roundup. My heart stopped when I saw the soldiers take hold of Theo. But there was nothing I could do.

"The next day, the soldiers carried out everyone's possessions from their homes—chairs, tables, beds with pillows and linens—and put them out on the streets. Precious photographs were scattered everywhere. There was no time, but I tried to gather up what keepsakes I could.

"I went there," continued Sophia, "to the prison. They were kept there in inhuman conditions until June eighth. Many people had nothing to wear except the nightclothes they were wearing at the time of their arrest. Then they, together with Greek and Italian prisoners, were transferred to Heraklion, to the cargo ship *Tanais*, headed for Piraeus, where they would have joined Jews from Corfu and Zakynthos, headed for Auschwitz. I managed to talk to Theo at Ayias Prison. He was happy his pregnant wife had escaped. That's all he cared about. It was too late for him and for the others around him, but everyone was happy to have Theo with them. It gave them hope. He was a born leader, a calming influence as they went to their deaths in the deep sea.

"It was June eighth, 1944. I remember that night the moon was shining. German soldiers herded members of the Cretan Jewish community—some two hundred and sixty-five Jews—along with some Christian resistance fighters and Italian prisoners, on board the *Tanais*, a requisitioned merchant vessel. At 2:31 on the morning of June 9th, while sailing in a convoy for Piraeus, thirty-three miles northeast of Heraklion, the *Tanais* was sighted, torpedoed, and sunk by the British submarine *HMS Vivid* off Santorini. The Jews trapped in its hold and all aboard went down to a watery grave. There was no counterattack. All that was found afterward was wreckage—fifteen floating pieces of wood of various shapes and sizes and twelve forty-gallon oil drums. Of the hundreds of victims, more than one hundred were children.

"For several years, there was a debate surrounding what caused the *Tanais* to sink. Many people believed the Germans had sunk the ship themselves, to exterminate the Jewish hostages; the truth of the matter is that the hostages were to be transported to concentration camps. For obvious reasons, the Germans always kept the cargo of their convoys a closely guarded secret. On the other hand, as part of military operations, the Allied Command made indiscriminate attacks on all German and Italian convoys."

"What exactly happened in those last hours of the *Tanais*?" Theia asked.

"We didn't know the details of the last hours of the *Tanais* and the fate of its human cargo for many years. What we did know is that the ship had been sunk on its way from Crete to Athens and that all aboard had perished. Tragically, it was only later learned that the *Tanais* had been sighted by a British submarine and sunk by its torpedoes.

"There's no doubt that the ultimate responsibility for the death of those on board lies with the Germans," said Wade. "That was their intention, whether they died because they were put out to sea under hazardous circumstances or would have perished at their ultimate destination."

"Theo went down with the ship?"

"What we did know is that the ship had been sunk and none of the prisoners survived," repeated Sophia. "Evidence surfaced later, from the Foreign Office in London, that showed the *Tanais* had been sighted by a British submarine and torpedoed, and that it sank within fifteen minutes. That's all it took to wipe out almost the entire Jewish population of Crete. I sometimes wonder if it was more humane to be blown up, if it was preferable to dying in Auschwitz, where they were headed.

"We hold an annual memorial service for the lost

Jews of Crete who perished on the *Tanais*, and we read out their names." Sophia led Theia and Wade down a hallway and to a memorial plaque inside the sanctuary, a shrine listing the names of the Jewish families that had boarded the *Tanais* and drowned on June 9, 1944.

"Avigades, Alhanati, Amar, Angel, Akkos, Attia, Belleli, Yannis, Dentes, Depas, Evlagon, Elhai, Fermon, Fortis, Frankis, Franco, Haskel, Hanen, Ishaki, Koen, Konen, Kounio, Leon, Minervo, Minionis, Molho, Osmos, Papousado, Politi, Sarphati, Savaton, Sereno, Sezana, Trevezi." Theia traced the names and settled finally on the last one, Frangos, her grandfather.

Here was a concrete tie to her past. She was the link to the next generation.

"June 9th, 1944," Theia repeated.

"Does that date mean something to you?" Sophia asked.

"Yes, it was the date my mother was born." Theia's grandfather had died the moment her mother was born. "My grandmother must have sensed something."

"I'll never forget the liberation," said Sophia. "German and Italian forces began withdrawing from the Greek mainland in late September of 1944 as Soviet forces advancing into southeastern Europe from the Ukraine threatened to cut them off. British forces then landed in October of 1944. By October thirteenth of the same year, the prefectures of Heraklion and Rethymnon were liberated, and Athens by October fourteenth. Occupation forces fell back to the north of Chania prefecture, where they remained until May of 1945.

"On May 9th, 1945, the German commander of the Fortress of Crete arrived in Heraklion by aircraft from Chania and was led to the Villa Ariadne at Knossos.

There he signed the unconditional surrender of the German troops. The document was to take effect as of 'ten o'clock Greenwich Mean Time on the tenth day of May 1945.' This was the final act of World War II in Europe."

"What about the other parts of Greece?" Wade wondered.

"It was the same story throughout Greece," said Sophia. "There are very many horrible incidents that happened on other Greek islands. Bulgarian and German soldiers dragged Jews off a passenger boat and massacred them, then sank the boat. Then they confiscated all the Jewish properties and possessions.

"The Jews of Ioannina were deported by the German Army on March 25th, 1944. Almost all of the people deported were murdered on or shortly after April 11th, 1944, when the train carrying them reached Auschwitz-Birkenau.

"The Nazis took control of Corfu in 1943. In early June of 1944, while the Allies bombed Corfu as a diversion from the landing in Normandy, the Gestapo rounded up the Jews of the city, temporarily incarcerated them at an old fort, and on June tenth sent them to Auschwitz. Very few survived. But two hundred out of about nineteen hundred managed to escape from the Nazis, and the local population provided them shelter and refuge.

"On July twenty-third, 1944, the 1,673 Jews of Rhodes—men, women, and children—were ordered to march to the port, where they were herded onto three crowded boats after being stripped of all their valuables and their identity papers. On that day, a centuries-old Jewish community ceased to exist.

"The crossing from Rhodes to mainland Greece took eight days. People died during the trip. After landing on Piraeus, Athens, and staying at the Haidari concentration camp, they were forced onto trains to Auschwitz, where most of them were murdered. There were only one hundred fifty survivors. Rhodes has a wonderful Jewish museum on synagogue grounds that explains everything.

"But there was good along with the bad," Sophia continued. "When the Jews of Salonika—that's what we call Thessaloniki in Judeo-Spanish—were rounded up for slave labor on July eleventh, 1942, the community paid two billion drachmas for their freedom. But still, fifty thousand people were sent to Auschwitz, and most of their six synagogues and schools were destroyed, along with the Jewish cemetery in the center of the city. Only nineteen hundred fifty survived."

Sophia related some other uplifting experiences. "The Grand Rabbi of Athens was summoned to the Department of Jewish Affairs and told to submit a list of names and addresses of members of the Jewish community. Instead, he destroyed the community records, thus saving the lives of thousands of Athenian Jews. He advised the Jews of Athens to flee or go into hiding. A few days later, the Rabbi himself was spirited out of the city by EAM-ELAS fighters and joined the resistance. EAM-ELAS helped hundreds of Jews escape and survive, many of whom stayed with the resistance as fighters and/or interpreters."

"What happened to the survivors?" asked Wade.

"Many emigrated to Israel or to the United States."

"How many Jews are left in Greece today?"

"About six or eight thousand people, mostly in Athens," Sophia replied. "Did you know that after the war Greece was the first country in Europe to give their Jewish community back the possessions of Jews killed by the Nazis in the Holocaust and the war? Some sixty to seventy thousand Greek Jews, or at least eighty-one percent of Greece's Jewish population, were murdered.

"But thousands of Jews like me were saved by the Greek Orthodox Church. Many Orthodox Christians risked their lives hiding Jews in their apartments and homes, despite threats of imprisonment. Although the Germans deported many Greek Jews, many others were successfully hidden by their Greek neighbors. Some, like me, managed to get forged identity cards with Christian aliases during the Occupation, after the Archbishop instructed the church to issue false baptismal certificates to all Jews who requested them. Even the Greek police ignored instructions to turn over Jews to the Germans."

"I've read that Neo-Nazi groups are surfacing in Greece," said Wade.

"That's a growing concern," admitted Sophia as she ended their tour in the cramped gift shop.

"Where did my grandparents' parents live?" Theia wanted to know.

"There's not a trace of it left. It was here in the old Jewish quarter, the *Ovraiki,* but back then everything was destroyed, if not by the bombing then by the German troops, including your father's studio. He was so proud of that studio. Which reminds me, I have something for you."

Sophie handed Theia a letter.

"After the war, a representative from the Museum

of Modern Art and from Marc Chagall delivered this letter for your grandfather. He asked about your grandfather, and I told him Theo had perished on the *Tanais*. He asked about your grandmother, with instructions to pass this on to any surviving relative. I never heard from Eleni, and until now no one has returned to claim it. I guess this letter belongs to you."

Theia's hand shook as she took the yellowing letter from Sophia's wrinkled hands and opened it. In it were specific instructions about who to contact at the National Museum of Modern Art in New York City about retrieving her grandfather's paintings. According to the letter, Theo's early paintings in France were sent to the museum in New York, where they still remained. She shared the letter with Wade. "After so many years, do you think any of these people are still there?"

"There's only one way to find out."

Theia grew excited. "His paintings! They have his paintings. I need to call my mother. I have to make a trip there immediately. When I get back to America, I'm going to make a stop in New York and meet with someone in this department to see if I can recover grandfather's paintings."

"I thought we were going to see more of Crete, perhaps visit Venice and Rome and Paris," Wade said.

"New York will be my next stop after I spend some time in Chania to learn about my heritage. I want to go to the places my grandparents went, experience their life here, find out more about the people, *my* people. You don't need to follow me, Wade. This is my journey."

Wade's eyes dimmed with disappointment. Then he raised his head. "I'm going to stay with you until you go back to the States."

"Whatever you wish. But I wouldn't want you to cut your vacation short on my account."

"Theia," he said, "this is more than a vacation to me." Theia turned away from him, all her energy focused on visiting her roots in Chania and on the upcoming trip to New York.

"Did you ever meet the other families besides the one in Atlanta?" Sophia wondered.

"Now that I know who they are, my mother and I will want to keep in touch. We're pretty much scattered, but I want us to get to know each other. I can't wait to talk to them and meet my people."

"Of course your grandmother, she was like a mother to them on their perilous journey. She saved their lives. All of the other families have been back to Crete for a visit."

"I guess my grandmother couldn't face returning without her husband. You've been so helpful and so very kind. Please keep the pictures safe."

Sophia promised she would.

"You must be hungry by now," Sophia said. "I can recommend a fine restaurant. You can sample some of the local foods."

Wade jumped up. "I'm starving."

Theia laughed. "Tell us where we should eat, what sights we should see. We want to do everything. I want to walk where my grandparents walked, see the sights they saw, eat the food they ate, and just explore the town." Sophia listed some restaurants and sights to see, and Theia wrote the pertinent information in a notebook from her purse.

"You'll see old charming buildings that have been

restored as hotels, restaurants, shops, and bars," said Sophia. "But the most distinctive area is the harbor and the medieval lighthouse. Your grandfather loved to paint the seafront.

"Agriculture, mostly olive trees and citrus, and tourism are our two big sources of income. Other important products include wine, avocados, and dairy. Apart from the traditional ways of cultivation, some of the producers have concentrated on practicing new methods in order to promote organic food."

Theia hugged Sophia and thanked her. She wondered if this was possibly the last time she would see the woman alive.

A cat slipped by Theia and Wade as they left the synagogue, and Theia laughed. They looked at menus posted outside restaurants primarily serving seasonal products from natural sources. They picked up fresh fruit and dried fruit from the local market that also sold wild herbs and aromatic plants. They enjoyed the olive oil that was used in salads and in cooking. They ate appetizers and local specialties, drank red wine, and for dessert enjoyed yogurt, traditional honey pastries, and fresh fruit.

Together Theia and Wade strolled down picturesque Kondilaki Street, the main street of the Old Jewish Quarter, that started at the harbor and extended up to the southern walls of Chania's Old Town. It was wider than the other alleys of the quarter. Theia read from the guidebook: "The Venetians who built the city made this street wide enough so the carts that carried supplies and munitions from the ships could pass through the city toward the south city walls. During the summer, Kondilaki Street and the surrounding alleys are some of the busiest streets of the Old Town of Chania."

She pointed to the surrounding streets on the map of Chania's Old Town—Chalidon, Zambelious, Skoufon, and Portou.

"Tomorrow, we'll retrace my grandparents' paths," Theia promised. "Our first stop will be the beach."

Chapter Seven

Theia and Wade lay on beach towels, bodies lightly touching, soaking in the warm rays of the summer sun. Both wore sunglasses. Theia's face was also covered with a straw hat for extra protection.

Their tour guide had dropped them off for a picnic on a deserted cove in a private bay in Chania, near where Theia's grandparents used to live. She wondered if they had ever come here to be alone, if her grandfather had ever painted this exact scene. If Theo and Eleni had made love on this very spot. She'd dreamed of these sandy, secluded beaches, with their colored pebbles—Balos, Falassama, Elafonissi—before she ever knew they existed. She'd painted those beaches, too, without ever having seen them. She was determined to visit all the places her ya-ya had mentioned in her letters, all the places she had been with her lover, her husband, Theia's biological grandfather. She'd dreamed of a man, too. But she could never recall his face. He was an illusion.

Tomorrow, she was going to take her camera, capture the beach scenes as closely as possible, and start to bring her dreams to life on her sketch pad. And now she had a face to put with the man in her dreams. Wade's face. But today was all about relaxing, letting the stress seep out of her body, unwinding, no thoughts of terrorists or world wars or the time when she and

Wade would have to part. She knew that day was coming soon. She'd already begun pulling away from Wade in her mind, and then she would have to let him go physically. She'd started at the synagogue, when she announced she was going on alone to New York. She would have loved to have his company, but nothing permanent could come of their relationship, so it was better to let him go now.

Theia removed her hat and looked through her giant sunglasses at the crystal blue waters of the paradise in front of her. She wriggled her toes in the soft sand and closed her eyes. She wore a white two-piece bathing suit to show off what few curves she had, and she'd finished off her outfit with gold strappy sandals, which would kill her ankle but exuded sex appeal, she hoped. She had to admit she'd wanted to look appealing for Wade, even though she and Wade could never end up together. He was wrong for her in every possible way. She removed her sunglasses, stole a look at Wade, and closed her mouth around her teeth, a fallback habit. The pull was strong.

"Don't close your mouth, Theia."

"There's an ugly space between my teeth. I was born with it. Now that I know my grandfather had that same space, I am starting to get used to it."

"That space drives me insane. I love that space. Open up and let me look at you."

"Like a dentist or a horse trader?" Theia wrinkled her nose.

"I would prefer like a lover. I adore every part of your body. You are perfection."

"I hardly have any breasts. I'm too thin. Wait until you see."

"I can't wait."

"The view is breathtaking," said Theia, suddenly sitting up and studying the particular blue of the sea and the stark white sand and the cliffs. "I can't wait to sketch it. I wonder if my grandfather sat in this exact same place with my ya-ya, and now I am seeing what he saw, feeling what he felt."

"The view is breathtaking, I agree," said Wade, his eyes focused solely on Theia. "Sketching is not what I had in mind. What are you feeling, Theia? Can you tell me?"

Theia turned toward Wade and pushed the hat back over her face.

"Don't be shy."

Theia shrugged.

"And don't be dismissive. I'm serious, Theia."

She pulled the hat from her face but didn't answer his question except to say, "I'm hungry."

"So am I, but not for food." Wade looked searchingly into Theia's wide eyes. He let out a breath. "You look frightened. You're not ready. All right, we will take this slowly. I could eat something. I had the hotel pack us a nice picnic lunch. I specifically asked for baklava. You said you liked sweets, so dessert first." He rooted around in the basket and came up with a sticky piece of baklava, which he unwrapped and fed her with his fingers. His hands were shaking.

"Sweet," she said, licking her lips to wipe off the taste of honey.

"Here, let me," Wade offered.

She detected a fierce hunger in his eyes. He would not wait much longer before he pounced.

He dipped his head, as the sun beat down on them,

and licked the sweet, papery-thin crumbs off her mouth and then pressed his lips to hers, warmth to warmth.

Her whole body was on fire. Now that he'd sampled her lips, she wanted more. She looked around. They were the only ones on the beach, as promised.

"We're completely and utterly alone here," Wade said, reading her thoughts. "The concierge said this beach was secluded, nudism friendly, even."

"N-nudism friendly?"

"Yes," said Wade, removing his sunglasses and throwing them carelessly on the towel. "There's not much time," he grunted.

"Time for what?"

"To make you fall in love with me."

Theia inched away from Wade.

"Where are you going?" asked Wade, gently picking up Theia's bare foot to examine it, rubbing it and kissing her toes. "How's your ankle?"

She shivered at his touch, although the air, as well as the sand and the sun, was warm.

"Much better."

"It's healing nicely. But you're not listening to my advice about wearing flats." He inclined his face toward the utterly sexy, utterly unsensible, gold, strappy, heeled sandals she'd brought to the beach.

"I thought we were going to explore Balos," Theia said, in an effort to change the subject.

"Too crowded for what I had in mind."

"And what did you have in mind?" Theia asked tentatively, rubbing her middle finger across her mouth to hide her teeth. "A little Wade in the water?"

"Cute, but no. What I had in mind to do to you the moment I laid eyes on you."

"And what is that?" she whispered, her eyes fluttering dangerously.

"You're flirting with me, you little devil," he said.

Theia smiled. Her body shook in anticipation, and she inched closer to Wade.

"Theia." He sighed, and she nestled into him, signaling her acceptance. "Do you want me as much as I want you?"

Theia's heart beat madly. Her breath came in short hitches. She reached out tentatively to touch Wade's hairy chest, rubbing his warm skin in a circular motion.

He unfastened her bathing suit top and freed her breasts. Her nipples hardened.

She wanted him to love her, but she could tell he needed a sign that she was ready.

Theia sighed and pushed his head down toward her breasts.

"Don't stop, please," she pleaded.

"I couldn't if I wanted to. I'm on fire—or else it's the sun."

"Then I am on fire, too."

Wade kissed her, and he couldn't stop kissing her. It was a miracle. They came together in a passionate embrace. Then he traced his fingers down her body and inside her bathing suit bottom. She arched her back.

"You're so soft."

Her body thrashed.

He kissed her again, for a long time, until she lost control.

"Come here, sweetheart." He slid her body under his and traced kisses all along and down her stomach, increasing the pressure and rhythm of his fingers.

Her lips were swollen, and she opened her legs,

indicating she was ready for him.

He moved inside her with swift strokes. Then he wrapped his hands around her bottom and hammered into her. "You're so tight."

"T-this is my f-first time," Theia stuttered. She reached out to touch him between her legs to indicate her pleasure.

"Theia?" he shouted hoarsely. "Do you want me to stop?"

"I might have to kill you if you do."

He relaxed and continued thrusting in and out, firm but gentle.

Theia climaxed.

"Oh, God," yelled Wade, and they went over the edge together. For a long time neither of them spoke.

"Wow," breathed Theia. "Just wow."

Wade sat up and looked at Theia. "You liked it?"

"It was nice."

"Nice, like tea time is nice?"

"Well, yes, soothing and relaxing. Theia time."

"I suppose next time I want to make love to you, I can say, "Would you like some tea?"

When she lay in his arms afterwards, she smiled and said, "Why do men in the movies always say, 'Oh, God,' after they make love?"

Wade laughed. "We say it in real life, too. Maybe because we're so close to heaven. This place is paradise, and so are you." He wrapped his arms around Theia and whispered, "Why didn't you tell me this was your first time? You really haven't slept with anyone before?"

"I was waiting for the right one."

"Am I the right one?"

"No, you're completely wrong."

"How can you be so sure?"

"The man I am going to marry will be Greek, and Jewish."

"Well, sometimes we don't get what we want, but we get what we need."

"Is that right?"

"Just so you know," Wade stated, "I'm not going anywhere."

Theia sat up and fastened her bathing suit top. She wasn't ready for this conversation.

"Suddenly, I'm starving. What else do you have in that basket?"

"Sandwiches, wine, a Greek salad, of course, and some more baklava for my insatiable goddess."

"I'm not insatiable," Theia protested.

"Then you put on a pretty good act. Let's go swimming, and then we'll eat."

"That's a great idea. This beach is amazing. I can't wait to get into the water."

"And I can't wait to get you into the water," Wade teased.

"Why is that?"

"If I keep you in the ocean, fighting the waves, then baking out in the sun all day, your body all warm and drowsy, you'll be too exhausted to put up a fight when I want to make love to you again in our air-conditioned hotel room on crisp, clean, white sheets."

Theia laughed. "You planned this all out."

"Is my plan beginning to work?"

"I think so." Theia felt relaxed and satiated. She was definitely loosening up.

Wade grabbed Theia's hand, and they ran down the

sandy beach and splashed into the water, laughing like children.

Drying off on the shore after their swim, they shared a delicious lunch. Theia was so full she didn't think she could move an inch.

"The driver will be back soon, so we'd better start packing up," said Wade. "Tomorrow we'll take the ferry to Balos Beach. Then I'll have to share you publicly."

"Not just yet. Let's play, 'If I were to die tomorrow,'" suggested Theia when they were both cocooned in their towels.

"How does that morbid little game work?"

"If I were to die tomorrow, I'd like to see one of my grandfather's paintings first."

Wade paused. "And if I were to die tomorrow, I would like to know what it feels like to make love to Theia again?"

"Yes, like that." Theia nodded.

"Like this?" Wade covered Theia's body and placed a soft kiss on her warm lips.

"Mmmm," she murmured, responding to his kiss. "Exactly like this."

"I like this game," Wade said.

Theia sat up and disentangled her body from Wade's. "But it's just a game. It's not reality. I am anxious to get to New York to inquire about my grandfather's paintings. I'm afraid I have to cut our trip short."

"Theia," Wade protested. "You're not even giving us a chance. You're running hot and cold. One minute you're in my arms, making love to me. The next, you want to hop away like a frightened rabbit. What are you afraid of?"

Theia lowered her eyes. "Of losing control."

"You're a strong woman. The odds of that happening are slim."

"I don't know," Theia said. "I think it's already happening."

Wade lifted Theia's chin and stared into her soul. "I need more time, Theia."

"I can't give that to you. I think our time together is done."

Chapter Eight

In the end, Wade convinced Theia to give him one more day.

"I'm desperate to see the Palace at Knossos," Wade said the next morning. "The site of the Minotaur legend."

"You're desperate?"

As a matter of fact, he was. Desperate to spend more time with Theia. He didn't care what they did or where they went as long as he could be with her. One more day to convince her they should be together permanently.

"I'm appealing to your Greek side."

"My Greek side is the only side I have."

"How can we leave Crete without seeing the ancient Palace at Knossos?" Wade reasoned. He handed Theia a pamphlet.

"Where did you get this?"

"The hotel office. There's a five-hour tour where we can discover the delights of the ancient Palace of Knossos. Listen to this." He grabbed the pamphlet back and began reading, his voice rising an octave.

" 'Follow in the footsteps of long-ago Minoan kings on this five-hour Knossos Crete tour. Travel by air-conditioned coach to the archaeological site of the Minoan Palace of Knossos, and tour the remains dating to the second century BC. Explore what were the royal quarters, storerooms, and Central Court of the palace, the power base of Europe's first civilization; and hear about the mythical Minotaur that roamed a labyrinth here as your guide explains the site's history. Finish with free time for lunch and a coach tour of Crete's capital, Heraklion.'

"There's an expert guide," Wade added, in an attempt to strengthen his case. "It says we can learn about Greek mythology and Minoan culture while walking through the Central Court, and discover sites like the Throne Room and Grand Staircase on the palace tour.

" 'We begin our experience with a pickup from our Crete hotel,' " read Wade, sounding like some game show host announcing the prizes hiding behind Door Number One. " 'Hop inside your coach and enjoy the scenic ride to Knossos, the world-famous site of a Minoan Palace that was later abandoned. On arrival, hop out of your coach and pay the entrance fee to the archaeological site.' "

"Pay the entrance fee?" Theia scowled. "That's not included in the price of the tour? That doesn't seem right."

"I will pay our entrance fee." Wade continued his reading. " 'Then, head inside to explore the buildings and ruins, many of them partially reconstructed by British archaeologist Sir Arthur Evans in the early 1900s. Follow your guide around the excavations and learn how the palace served as the ceremonial and administrative hub of Crete's Minoan culture, considered to be Europe's oldest civilization. Inspect the once-lavish royal quarters, treasuries, and storerooms, and admire the restored frescoes that depict long-ago scenes of Minoan life. See the Central Court, Grand Staircase, and Throne Room, and as you stroll, hear about the mysterious Greek legends associated with the palace, including the strange myth of the Minotaur—the half-man, half-bull said to have been imprisoned by King Minos within a labyrinth at the palace. After your tour, return to your coach and continue into Heraklion for a panoramic sightseeing tour and free time for lunch (own expense).' "

"Own expense? What kind of a cut-rate tour is this?"

"At my expense," Wade corrected. "This day is all on me. But listen, there's more. 'Pass top Heraklion attractions such as Koules Venetian Fortress, Lions Square, and the Church of St. Titos as your guide recounts historical anecdotes about the city and its time under Venetian rule between the thirteenth and seventeenth centuries. With your sightseeing over, your tour ends with a hotel drop-off.' And, oh, I almost forgot. The man at the front desk said it included a tour of a winery/olive oil store and time in Heraklion to walk around, eat lunch—at my expense, of course, as previously stated—and go to the Archaeological Museum. How does that sound?"

Theia shook her head. "Wade, I'm supposed to be at the airport this afternoon."

"Well, you'll just have to change your flight, because I already bought our tickets."

"You what?"

"I thought, What self-respecting Greek could visit Crete and not see the Palace at Knossos?"

"Wade." Theia placed her hands on her hips in an intractable stance. "You're not playing fair. Do you mean to tell me you'd rather traipse around in the hot sun all day?"

"No. I'd rather spend the day in bed making love to you in our air-conditioned hotel room," Wade said. "But I'll take what I can get."

"You're impossible."

"So you'll do it?"

"Did you really buy the tickets already?"

Wade pulled an envelope out of his pocket and produced them.

"One more day," Theia agreed. "But that's it."

Wade picked her up and twirled her around.

"You won't be sorry."

"I already am." Theia laughed.

"You admit you want to see this place."

"I do, but I also want to spend one more day with you."

Wade beamed and kissed Theia on the lips. She tasted like mint toothpaste. He would forever associate the taste of mint with Theia.

"Okay, then let's get ready, because it's almost pick-up time. We'd better eat something before we go. I'm sure breakfast is not included in this 'cut-rate tour,' as you call it. I just hope the bus doesn't break down."

****

The bus did break down, and they had to be picked up by another bus, an hour later. When they finally got to the Palace, hot, sticky, tired, and thirsty, Wade frowned.

"It certainly is ancient. It's just a bunch of rubble."

"Wade Bingham, use your imagination," Theia chided, enthralled. "Think what it must have been like. There, you can actually see the Minotaur up there on that wall. You see his horns?"

"I guess so."

"Stop sulking. Try to enjoy yourself. I love this. I'm going to sketch it when we get back to the hotel."

"How can I enjoy myself when I know this is the last day we're going to be together? We may never see each other again."

"Who knows what fate has in store for us? If we're meant to see each other again, then it will happen." Theia took Wade's hand. "Let's just enjoy this day together."

Chapter Nine

Theia felt the urge to paint something powerful and important to commemorate the sinking of the *Tanais*, something on the size and scale of Picasso's *Guernica*, an enormous mural-sized oil painting on canvas that measured about eleven feet tall and twenty-five feet wide, painted for the 1937 World's Fair in Paris.

She rejected Picasso's stark monochrome palette of black, white and gray, a matte house paint with the least possible gloss, rendered with the immediacy of a black-and-white photograph to depict the horror, misery, and devastation of the carpet bombing that destroyed Guernica. A German guidebook had called Picasso's mural, featuring a gored horse, a bull, a dismembered soldier, a grieving woman, and smoke and flames, a "hodgepodge of body parts. A nightmarish scene of chaos."

Picasso didn't witness Guernica firsthand. He never set foot in the country while painting it. In fact, after he painted the masterpiece, he never returned to Spain. He didn't go to work on the piece until May 1, 1937, three weeks before the exhibit was scheduled to open, and he finished it in just over a month, on June 4, 1937, after only thirty-five days of work. Theia would need more time than that.

Like Picasso, Theia hadn't experienced the horror of the sinking of the *Tanais* firsthand. No matter, the destruction was etched in her brain and trapped in her dreams. The pain and the loss were palpable.

At night, Theia was haunted by the thought that her grandfather and the other Jews from his birthplace had perished at sea. What had her grandfather's final moments looked like? If she were to paint them, they would be dark, black, devoid of light and hope. She imagined how frightened the passengers must have been, trapped in the ship's hold, body stashed against body, no room to breathe, before they were bombarded and drowned in a mass grave. Gasping for breath, their lives choked off, flailing in the ocean, surrounded by the inky, murky darkness of the sea. Children blown from their mothers' arms. Lovers and newlyweds torn apart. Or maybe they had perished instantly, with no time to say their goodbyes. Maybe they didn't even know their fate. But Theo knew what was in store for the group at the end of the journey. Death. He had seen it in France. Did he warn them? Did he have some plan in mind to save them? Either way was too horrifying to contemplate. She imagined her grandfather's last thought had been with Eleni and their child. A child he'd never live to see. Were his final thoughts regret that he didn't accompany her to America? She would never know.

Theia tossed and turned on the bed in the hotel room, tears streaming down her face, until she felt someone shaking her shoulder.

"Theia, wake up. You're having another bad dream."

Wade turned on the bedside light. "You're crying. Sweetheart, what's wrong?"

Theia wiped at her tears with the sheet and sniffled.

Wade was ready with a tissue. She'd forgotten where she was. That she was still here with Wade, in his bed in the hotel. She hadn't let him make love to her again, although he'd coaxed and cajoled her all evening. She'd almost capitulated. With a great day at the beach and an afternoon of sightseeing at the harbor, they had grown closer. Then the tour of the Palace at Knossos. Her feelings for Wade were growing. With each passing day, she was afraid she could no longer resist him. He had called her sweetheart. Things had gone too far, too fast. It had to stop. Perhaps the intensity of their relationship had been ratcheted up by their life-or-death experience at the hotel in Florence. Or it might be the fact that they were out of the U.S.; therefore none of the real-world relationship rules applied. Or was it the warmth of Wade's body stretched out in the sunlight? Their flame was bright, maybe too bright to last.

"It's nothing."

"It's not nothing. You're shaking. Please tell me what the dream was about."

Trying to put her thoughts into words was impossible. She wanted Wade's strong arms around her, but she had to learn to stand on her own. She'd already told him she was flying out in the morning to board a plane for New York City.

"You don't have to worry about me," she said, surfacing from her nightmare.

"It's too late for that," Wade said. "Theia, can we talk?"

"I need to sleep. I have a plane to catch in the morning."

"I can go with you."

"I don't want you to."

"You're being stubborn," Wade said.

"Do you want to pick a fight on our last night together?" she challenged.

"I don't want it to be our last night together."

"Go back to sleep," she said, turning away from him to face the wall, when everything in her wanted to turn toward him.

Wade pulled the covers up to his chin and turned toward the bathroom. "You're making a mistake."

"Well, it's my mistake to make."

They slept, or didn't sleep, in silence the remainder of the night.

Theia studied the full moon outside her window. She would paint that moon one day. And one day, when it stopped hurting, she would paint Wade. She had only known him for a short while, but in that time she had grown to depend on him, to need him, maybe even to love him.

Fresh tears slipped silently down her face.

Chapter Ten

Wade woke to bright sunlight streaming in the window of their hotel. He stretched out an arm and patted the other side of the bed.

"Theia?"

When no one answered, he thought she must already have gone down to breakfast. He closed his eyes, hoping to catch a few more minutes of sleep, until the truth hit him between the eyes like a two-by-four. He bolted out of bed, grabbed his watch from the bedside table, and then cursed. Maybe he could still catch her. Then his head fell back onto the pillow. No, she didn't want to be caught. He'd fallen asleep, he'd overslept, and she was gone, forever. It was too late. He could kick himself.

He'd offered to drive her to the airport, to wait with her for her plane, so they could spend the last few precious moments together, but she had steadfastly refused. He'd spent most of the night looking at her, drinking her in, memorizing her features, and he'd tried to stay awake until morning. But he must have dozed off, and she'd made her getaway, like a thief, in the middle of the night, a thief who'd stolen his heart.

She'd left him. He could almost calculate the odds. That's what women did. He'd had plenty of experience with that. He should be used to it by now. Dispirited, he plodded into the bathroom. Her towel was hanging on the rack. He sniffed it. He could still smell her. He'd marveled at the way she used the towel to wrap around her damp head after she'd washed her fragrant hair. It was some kind of magical turban swirl that women did. His mother and his sisters could do it, too, and, of course, his ex-fiancée. It was in the women's handbook of wondrous things that men could never hope to imitate or understand. He walked to the closet to confirm his worst fears. Her suitcase and all her clothes were gone.

Wade showered and dressed. He felt like a ship adrift. He didn't think he could take a step forward. He hadn't even gotten a chance to say goodbye. He couldn't believe he wasn't going to see Theia's beautiful face again.

Then he saw what was on the desk.

He picked up the thick, creamy piece of paper torn out of Theia's sketch pad. She must have done it in the middle of the night—a sketch of him, only a pencil sketch, but it captured him. Theia was truly talented. She'd signed the sketch at the bottom. *Love, Theia.* And he realized that he did love Theia. He wished she had left him a sketch of herself, but Theia wouldn't have thought to do that. She didn't have a vain bone in that magnificent body of hers. She had been thinking of him at the end. But why hadn't she taken his likeness with her? Maybe she didn't need a reminder of his face. He could certainly never forget her. He hoped he could conjure up her face, and her gravelly voice, long after she was gone.

He looked through the photos on his cell phone. At least he'd have a record of those memories. She'd taken his address so she could mail him a check for the expenses he'd fronted her. But he'd never thought to get her phone number or address. He thought there would be more time. Shoulders slumped, he packed up his clothes, pulled his suitcase out of the room, and checked out of the hotel. Where should he go? What should he do? He needed a plan.

The first item on his agenda was to drive back to the synagogue. He had no idea where Theia lived. He knew she was from Atlanta, but Atlanta was a big place. Sophia, the woman in the church, said Theia's mother had called her to announce her daughter's arrival. He would get her number. After New York, Theia would no doubt head home. She was what, 22? Maybe 24? She'd just graduated college. It made sense that she'd still be living with her parents. Why hadn't he thought to get her phone number? What had they talked about? Everything. Big picture things. Mundane things. Hopes and dreams. But he had forgotten to get the critical details.

When he got to the synagogue, Sophia greeted him warmly. "Where's Theia?"

"Gone, but I need to get her mother's phone number."

Sophia went into the office and came out with a phone number written on a piece of paper. She smiled, planted a kiss on his cheek, and said, "Go after her."

"Is it that obvious?"

"To me it is. You were sparring and stumbling all over each other like a couple of playful puppies, but love was written all over your faces. It was the same with Theo and Eleni."

"Thank you, Sophia." Wade pulled out a handful of bills and placed them in the Tzedakah bowl.

Should he continue on with his vacation? Get her email address and send her selfies of him alone in Santorini and Mykonos and Athens and Rome and Venice, saying, "Wish you were here," and, "Missing you"? Theia would dismiss the snaps and call him a dork. As far as he was concerned, there was no place like Crete on earth and no woman on earth like Theia. Should he go back to San Francisco, back to his job, back to his life, which he'd thought was enough before he met Theia? But now that he'd been with her, he knew it would never be enough.

This was a siege, like the one in Florence, and he was going to fight for her and never give up. Not until she was in his arms again. And when that happened, he was never going to let her go.

But how was he going to win her back? Should he watch *My Big Fat Greek Wedding*? Study Greek mythology? Greek literature? Learn to be more Greek? Study Hebrew? How was he going to accomplish that Herculean feat? Right now he was like Sisyphus, ceaselessly, futilely, hopelessly rolling a rock to the top of a mountain, only to have the stone fall back down on him. He had met his Venus and the gods were playing their mind games.

Wade made a few phone calls. He was headed for Atlanta. And he was going to wait there until Theia returned. If he had to wrestle with any of her Greek beaus, he would. If he had to compose love letters, he would do that, too. He would do anything to win her back. She was that important to him.

Part Three
The Letters

"In the arts, as in life, everything is possible provided it is based on love."

~Marc Chagall

Marilyn Baron

Chapter Eleven

Dearest Carolina and Theia,

If you're reading this letter, I am no longer on this earth. I'm sorry to say I've kept some secrets from you, things you both had a right to know, but things I couldn't bear to talk about or think about. There is no other way to say this but to say it.

Of course you both know I was from Greece and I left Crete before the end of the war. But what you don't know, Carolina, is that your father, and Theia, your Papou, was not who you think he was. I was already married when I came over from Crete. Married and pregnant with you, Carolina. It was during the war, and my husband was Theo Frangos, a handsome and talented young artist who studied with Chagall. He was the love of my life.

Theia, you have always reminded me of him, and every time I slipped up and mentioned that you resembled your Papou, you would laugh and wrinkle your nose and say, "But Papou is bald and fat and has a hairy beard. I don't look anything like him." But you were the image of your real grandfather. You have his eyes. And that space between your teeth.

And you obviously inherited his talent. I have arranged for you to take a trip to Italy for your college graduation present because every artist should visit Italy. Your grandfather would have liked that.

After your trip, I hope you'll visit Crete, my birthplace and the birthplace of your real grandfather. Theo and I were childhood sweethearts. We were in love, and we got married. He wanted me to leave Crete when the Germans arrived, but I told him I wouldn't leave, that things were not that bad. But then they were, and finally, after years of occupation, it was too late to get out. My Theo was part of the resistance. He arranged for me to get out and to take with me five otherwise unaccompanied children, on the last boat out of Crete. He saved me and our child, Carolina, and five other children, but it was too late for him.

Because I was pregnant, I agreed to go, and he promised me he would follow. But, in times of war, we cannot always keep our promises. He was caught in Chania, our home, and rounded up with the rest of the Jewish community, all put on a boat bound to Auschwitz. The boat, the Tanais, *was sunk, and there were no survivors. I still blame myself for his death. If I had only gone with him when he wanted to leave, our lives would have been so different.*

I was grieving, but I had you to look out for, Carolina, and so I moved on with my life. Theia, your father was one of the children I brought out of Crete, and he and your mother eventually married and were happy. The other children were taken in by families around the world—in South Africa, South America, Los Angeles, and Australia. I've kept in touch with them over the years, and we've exchanged pictures. Some of them returned to Crete, but I couldn't bear to go back without my Theo. I would like you to know them, too.

Theia, I want you to make a pilgrimage to Crete, to the synagogue, and place these pictures on the Memory

Wall there. Although Crete's Jewish population was wiped out, we survived and thrived elsewhere, and raised families, and these pictures are a testament to that.

My hope is that you will find a trace of your grandfather, explore your talent, become a great artist like him, and like your mother, marry a Greek man and find happiness and thrive and survive. Please forgive me for keeping this secret.

All My Love,
Ya-Ya

Theia looked at her mother through tear-laden eyes.

"I had no idea," Carolina said. "All this time, and I thought your Papou was my father."

Theia shook her head. "My grandfather was an artist. I wish I could see something he painted."

"We'll have to look into this," Carolina said. "I never heard of the *Tanais*. My real father died during the war. That's unbelievable."

"Look at this picture, Mama. This must be him. He was very handsome."

"Theia, he looks just like you. You even have the same space between your teeth, the space you always hated. And you have his beautiful eyes. I always wondered where those came from."

Theia touched her tongue to her teeth, a familiar habit. "I wish she were still here so I could ask her some questions."

"Remember you told me you saw a man at the foot of the bed when Ya-Ya died?"

"Yes, it was this man in the picture. And he was young, like he is in this wedding picture."

"Imagine that," Carolina said. "I knew about the trip your grandmother was planning for you. She gave me all the paperwork. It was supposed to be a surprise for your birthday. I want you to go."

"Don't you want to go, to see where she was born, where your parents were born?"

"I need to talk to your father, but no, you go and represent the family. Let's look through these pictures and letters and see what else we can learn."

Theia emptied the box. There were more pictures of a young Ya-Ya with a handsome young man in wedding attire, family pictures in a faraway place that Theia had never seen before. And a packet of letters.

Theia wiped her eyes and started reading aloud to her mother, who could hardly compose herself. Theia picked up one of the letters. "Here's one from Theo, from your father, to Ya-Ya, written from France in 1940."

Dearest Eleni,

They're rounding up Jews in France. You need to get ready to leave. I know you are thinking that nothing like that is happening or can ever happen in Greece.

Not yet. But how do we know what will happen? Marc's getting out with his family, but it is almost too late. He's offered me a way out, through Marseilles. He's agreed to take my paintings with him to New York City. But I told him I won't leave without you.

And you have told me you will never leave. I'm coming home. Maybe I can convince you it is too dangerous for us to stay.

Your Theo

"And here's another, from Ya-Ya, written to Theo from Atlanta," Theia said.

My Dearest Theo,

I haven't heard from you in a while, and I know it is impossible to send letters during the war. I don't even know where you are, off in the mountains fighting, or in Chania. I know one thing—wherever you are, I am with you and you are with me.

I have news, the best news. Our daughter was born at 2:31 on the morning of June 9. I woke up sweating. I couldn't breathe. The air was stale. The walls were closing in on me. I felt like I was drowning, but you were there with me and you held my hand and spoke of your love. And you said I must live. I must have been dreaming, because when I woke up you were gone.

But the family that took us in got me to the hospital, and I gave birth to a beautiful little girl. She's a knockout. She looks just like you. She has all her fingers and toes and a beautiful head of dark hair. I wonder if she will be an artist like you. I can't wait for you to see her. Come to us as soon as you can. The family that took us in also took a boy from our town, one of the ones I was traveling with, so our children will grow up together. The man is a very respected man in our synagogue. He is very wealthy, older than us, but he has given me and now Carolina, your daughter, our own room, a home while we wait for you.

His wife is very ill and will probably die soon, so I've been helping out as I can with the cooking, cleaning, and mothering the little boy I brought over— and, of course, our Carolina. Now that I have the little ones to care for, I am always exhausted. The one thing I live for is the day when you come back to us. I should not have gone without you.

The newspapers here update us on the war, but we

have no idea when it will be over. Come to us as soon as you can. I love you.

Always,
Your Shining Star

Theia held her hand over the letter. The way her ya-ya signed the letter triggered another memory. Her grandfather, step-grandfather now, used to call himself her grandmother's "Constellation Prize." She wondered whether he knew about Theo. He must have. If Theo called his wife "My Shining Star," then maybe that's why Papou referred to himself as a Constellation Prize, meaning he was the consolation prize compared to her first husband. Her grandparents hadn't been very affectionate, but somehow they had four children together. It was obvious her grandfather—her step-grandfather—worshipped the ground his wife walked on, but Ya-Ya was more reserved when they were together. Theia couldn't recall them touching or leaning into each other, or exhibiting any signs of being in love.

What she did remember was that whenever they went anywhere, whether to synagogue, out to dinner or a movie, or on vacation, it was like moving a small town. Still, she had only happy memories of her family. Her grandmother's memories must have been bittersweet, if she thought of all the other children she could have had with Theo.

Theia and her mother read the remaining letters, the correspondence that spoke of love and passion, letters from Ya-Ya to Theo and letters Ya-Ya had saved from Theo, describing his time with the great artist, his mentor, Marc Chagall in France.

"This is the last one, Mom." Theia held her mother's hand while she read it aloud. "It's from 1944."

My darling Theo,

This is the last letter I will write to you. I will not mail it because now that you're gone it is undeliverable. We just heard the news about the Tanais *and read the names of the families that went down with the ship—my parents, all of our friends. But when I read your name, I didn't believe it, and then I screamed and screamed and would not come out of my room. Mr. Constas tried to comfort me, but I could not be comforted. I think baby Carolina must have sensed something was wrong, because she wouldn't stop crying, and she wouldn't take the breast.*

I wouldn't eat and couldn't sleep, and I wanted to die with you. But then who would care for our precious Carolina? Now she is my only tie to you.

Eventually, I came out of my grief. I will never fully recover, because you are my life, and when you died, you took my happiness with you. Life for me will never be the same. There is no hope, nothing to look forward to. I am just an empty shell. Only the thought of Carolina keeps me tethered to this earth because she is a part of you.

Mr. Constas has been a godsend. He's always there when I need him, like a father, very dependable and kind. He walks Carolina every night, and he bottle feeds her because I am too bereft and my milk has dried up. He knows he is losing his wife, so he understands my despair.

I have to stop now. Carolina is crying. So am I.

"It stops here and then continues one year later," said Theia.

Dearest Theo,

Before she died, Mr. Constas's wife, Anastasia,

came to me. She knew she was dying and so did her husband. But she wanted him to be happy and not mourn her after she was gone.

"But wait… Here's a letter from Papou's first wife. It's to Ya-Ya from Anastasia Constas, the woman who died. Here's what it says."

I am coming to you, Eleni, because I see how lonely you are and how you mourn your beloved Theo. And you have a child to take care of. I do not wish that loneliness on my husband. Soon I will leave this world, and I want to make sure I leave him and Bennie in good hands. In your hands. I know this will sound strange for me to be giving my blessing for another woman to occupy my husband's bed, but I have come to know you. You are a good woman and a good mother and a good friend. So I trust my husband's happiness to you. Promise me you will make him happy.

You may have your doubts. That's only reasonable, but first, let me tell you a little about my husband that you may not know, so that you will understand what a good man he is. A man worthy of your love. A man who will give you a good life, and yes, even passion, although I know your first instinct will be to resist because you don't think you deserve happiness or that you will ever find it again. But you do deserve to be happy, and you will be happy again.

Ari grew up in Crete, and he and his brother came to the United States when Ari was fifteen. It was the 1920s, before you were even born, and at that time they left for economic reasons. He began by repairing shoes, and eventually he opened a shoe repair shop like his father had on Crete. His brother, who was apprenticed to a tailor in Crete, went into the leather business. They both opened up shops but lost everything in the Depression. But he kept working, doing anything and everything to earn a little money, and eventually he became the success he is today.

When it was time for him to marry, Ari took a boat back to Crete to find a Greek wife, which, as you know, is the Sephardic custom.

In my generation and my parents' generation, we were encouraged to marry Sephardic. Ari spoke predominantly Spanish; his family was one of those who left Spain in the fifteenth century because of the Inquisition. He also speaks Ladino, which you speak, a collection of Turkish and Hebrew words, so you already have that in common.

So my Ari came back to Crete to find a wife, and he set his sights on me. And you should know that when my husband makes up his mind, he is a force to be reckoned with. He saw me, and that was it for him. I was just eighteen, and I was not as convinced. My mother had a nice house where she lived with her sister and me. But she had already made a match for me with a wealthy banker in his fifties, an older man I definitely did not want to marry. So I saw my opportunity to get out of an arranged marriage—Ari courted me, and I agreed to marry him, and he finally won my mother over. Believe me, I made the right decision to go to America and not marry that banker.

We went back to America and landed at Ellis Island. That's where Ari had first heard of Greek cluster settlements in the South, in cities like Montgomery, Tampa, and Atlanta. News of the Southern communities spread by word-of-mouth. When we returned to Atlanta, we became founding members *of our Sephardic synagogue in the city.*

Now, to look at my Ari, you wouldn't know he was such a good lover. But let me assure you, Eleni, he is. It came as a total surprise to me, too. But he has a very big sexual appetite, a lot of staying power, and woman to woman, will more than satisfy you. As a matter of fact, before we left Greece for America, before he would agree to marry me, he wanted me to sample the goods, to make sure I would be happy. And I did and I was. Don't think I couldn't see right through that hot-blooded Greek rascal. He wanted to sample the goods, too. So we had a feast. He bought two tickets on a freighter, we got on a boat in Crete and got to Italy, where we were detained for almost a month before we were allowed to go on to America.

Ari and I did make a trip back to Crete once, just before the war. Ari couldn't believe it when we saw how he and his brother and parents had lived in such a small stucco home. It had seemed so big before we moved to America. Where he had lived was an old house in a medieval city. The doorway was an archway no more than six feet tall. Ari is a big man, in more ways than one. He could barely fit through it.

Ari always said Crete was a nice place to live, that life moved slowly there. There was no hustle and bustle. It was an idyllic existence.

But here's what I do remember, as I'm sure you will too because we've talked about it. The old Venetian lighthouse in the old port of Chania, the ancient Minoan ruins, the peaceful hillside villages, and of course, the beaches. Crete is now for the tourists who come in droves on the cruise ships. Or people who visit the land of their ancestors. The children of the generation that was born there are dying off. There are only about twelve Jews left on the island. Crete would have been my home and yours. And now you must make a new home here in America, regrettably without your beloved Theo. I hope you will make a home with Ari.

Most everybody we knew back in Crete left before things started getting bad for the Jews in Greece, with all the anti-Jewish rules. I still remember hearing about the last boat out before the Nazis arrived. It was Ari who helped supply the money to get six children out of Crete, and that included you and your Carolina. Unfortunately, Ari and I could not have children. It was our greatest sorrow. But we adopted Bennie when he came over, and we kept you and Carolina in our house also. Having you and Carolina and Bennie with us has brought us so much joy.

When we were first married, it was not unusual around our house for us to hear the phone ring. It would be a relative saying, "Hello, we're here from Crete, and we need a place to stay. We're in New York, and we'll be in town tomorrow." Ari would not turn anyone away. His door was always open. Shelter, food, money, advice—he gave them anything they needed and more. That is the kind of man he is. Generous to a fault, to friends and strangers.

So he's not a Greek god like your Theo. And now he's grown a paunch, is bald on top, and has sprouted hairs where there should be none. You, on the other hand, are a beautiful young woman, with soft skin and supple breasts. Don't doubt for a minute that he desires you. I've seen him looking at you when he thinks your head is turned and I'm not looking. Who can blame him? But you won't mind him in your bed once the lights are out. He is still a tiger. You may think I'm a crazy old woman who is trying to talk you into my husband's bed. But I am a woman who loves her husband and wants him to be as happy as he has made me. Life has dealt us a bad hand, as it has dealt you. What is that expression? If you are handed a lemon, make lemonade? Together, you and Ari can make lemonade, make love, and make each other happy. You can warm his bed and he will warm your heart.

It is for these reasons that I recommend him to you. Woman to woman. Please give him a chance. You won't regret it.

"And now I'll continue Ya-Ya's letter to Theo," Theia said.

Theo, the wife of my benefactor, Mr. Constas, died almost a year ago. It is so sad around the house. He misses her so, the way I miss you. He putters around the house in a depressed state. But lately, I notice he has come out of his shell. I see the way Mr. Constas looks at me, like I am the moon and the stars, like I am something precious. I am not anyone's shining star if I am not yours. I will never stop loving you, never stop wanting you, dreaming of you, hoping for a miracle that someday we will be together. The other day, Mr. Constas kissed me. It was not a rough kiss. It was a soft, gentle kiss, but a hungry kiss. I was not surprised. I see him watching me when he thinks I am not looking. I know he has feelings for me. But he treats me like Venetian glass. He knows if he moves too fast, I will surely break.

He has a beard, and when he kisses me, it tickles. You remember how I hate men with beards. But this is the reality of life, Theo. He is so lonely, and so am I, and he is such a good man. He's asked me to marry him, and he says he will spend the rest of his life doing everything he can to make me happy, and that he will love Carolina like his own, which he already does. You should see them together. Carolina adores him. She tugs on his beard and laughs so. He doesn't know I will never be happy again. I try to remember the last time I was truly happy, and that was when I was in your arms. He promises he will provide for me and Carolina, and of course he has adopted Bennie, one of the boys I brought over to America, and he will give us all a good life.

He knows I cannot love him the same way I love you. I cannot give him my whole heart, although I have given him my body. I've told him all about you. What am I to do? I wish you were here to tell me. I hope you will forgive me, but without some help I cannot go on.

I am a terrible woman. When he takes me in his arms, I sometimes pretend he is you, and that it is you touching me, kissing my lips and my breasts, caressing my body. I can tell it makes him happy because he thinks finally I have come around and that I want him as a woman wants a man. I want to scream because he is not you, my darling, but my body betrays me and responds as if to your touch. Sometimes I can't bear to have him touch me in the same places you touched me. Ours is not an easy love, not like it was between us. There is no fire, no passion. I do not live for him like I lived for you. But I am weak, and I'm afraid I could not live in this strange country without him or someone.

Please forgive me, my love. I feel I cannot go on unless I lock you away, with all our dreams and desires, all the thoughts of our lives together or thoughts of the life we will never have. I cannot think of you, cannot think of Chania, cannot bear to discuss any of it. I will put all your letters away and try to make a new life for myself and for Carolina.

I know I will have to forget about you and where I came from if I am to be a proper wife to my new husband.

Yours always, Eleni

Theia's mother wiped her eyes. "I had no idea how difficult it was for her. I thought she loved my father, your Papou. I thought he made her truly happy the way your father makes me."

"I'm sure she loved him in her way. But she couldn't forget her first love. I think she made the best life for herself and you that she could. I can hardly wrap my head around it. Papou was not my grandfather or your real father."

"No. But he was a good man. He took us in and supported us when we needed him. He was the only father I knew. According to this letter, I was born at the exact moment my real father perished on the *Tanais*. My mother wanted us to name you Theia. It must have been after her first husband."

"Remember Ya-Ya would look at me and say, 'You look just like your grandfather.' But I thought she was delirious. I looked nothing like Papou. Papou was fat, with a beard. I have the body of a boy. She said when she looked at my drawings they reminded her of her husband's drawings. But even Papou would admit he couldn't draw a straight line with a ruler.

"And then when she died, I held her hand and she said, 'Find your grandfather.' And I thought she was hallucinating, because Papou has been dead for so long.

What do you think she meant?"

"I think she meant that you should go to Crete, take the photographs she left you in her shoebox, find the synagogue, and deliver the pictures. My mother would never talk about her days in Crete, never mention them. The memories must have been too painful for her to bear. Maybe you can fill in the details.

"Your father and I adore each other, but my parents weren't very affectionate with each other, at least not in public. I always wondered why. Now it makes sense. I thought that in private they probably behaved differently. Your ya-ya was certainly fertile. They produced enough children. Those children didn't fall down from the sky. They weren't delivered by a stork. They came the natural way. She must have made her husband a very happy man, since he couldn't have children in his first marriage. Children are such a blessing. I don't know what I would do without you and the boys."

"Well, it works both ways, Mom. You are the best mother in the world." She hugged her mother.

"Thank you, Theia."

"Mom, look at these pictures," Theia said. "I didn't know Ya-Ya could smile."

"I rarely saw her smile, except at her children," her mother lamented.

"How could we not have known about all of this?"

"Whenever I talked to her about her past, she got so upset I dropped it. I wasn't going to get any answers from her. When I asked your Papou, he wasn't talking either. I hope you can find some answers when you go to Crete."

Chapter Twelve

When Theia arrived at the Museum of Modern Art in New York City, she was exhausted from the long plane ride and the crying jags triggered whenever she thought of the way she'd left Wade. She'd refused to let him take her to the airport. In fact, she'd snuck out before daylight, like a thief, without a final goodbye. Neither one of them had achieved closure.

"What will you do after I'm gone?" she'd asked him.

"Go home, I guess. I don't want to be here without you."

"I'm sorry, for everything."

"I'm not. I'm not sorry I met you, because I still think there's a chance for us."

"Wade, I can't deny my feelings for you. But with everything I've learned about my family history, I feel I have a duty, a responsibility to—"

"To marry a Greek man and have Greek children? Do you know how unrealistic that sounds? You can't just manufacture a man like that out of thin air."

"There are plenty of Greek men at my synagogue back home who are interested in me."

"So why didn't you marry any of them?"

"I was not interested in them then. But I am going to take a second look, now that I know more about my past."

"Why don't we visit Santorini?" Wade suggested. "I hear it's a beautiful island."

"Next you'll want to visit Athens, or Mykonos, and then, I suppose, Rhodes."

"They say all roads lead to Rhodes."

"That's Rome, and you know it." Theia suppressed a smile.

"Didn't you say your grandmother told you every artist should see Rome?" Wade countered. "We could go back to Italy."

Theia threw her hands up in frustration. "Stop! I will go back to those places, one day. But now there's something more important I have to do."

"One more day, Theia," Wade pleaded. "I just need one more day."

"You won't change my mind."

"I might."

"I'm anxious to see my grandfather's paintings."

"What if I changed my name to Socrates or Homer or Euripides?"

"That won't change the fact that you're not Greek."

"How about Aristotle? You could call me Ari. It sounds Israeli."

"That name is already taken. That was my Papou's name."

They had argued all night until they were both worn out. Though they shared the bed, Theia refused to let Wade touch her. If he did, she feared her willpower would dissolve. One kiss, one stroke of his fingers on her body, and she would give in. When he reached for her and tried to kiss her, in a last attempt to change her mind, she allowed him one long, slow kiss, and she almost relented. Her body hungered for his, but, reluctantly, and restlessly, she pulled away.

When the new day dawned, Wade was asleep. Theia had slipped out before sunup.

In New York, she'd spent the night at a small boutique hotel near the Museum of Modern Art and slept most of the next day away. But she was determined not to miss her late afternoon appointment with the woman who now headed the department that had issued the letter to her grandfather after the war.

Many different people had held that position since the nineteen-forties, but the office was currently under the authority of a young and very attractive, fashionably dressed woman who warmly welcomed her to MOMA.

"I was so excited to get your call, Miss Constas," said the curator, a Miss Farrah Stone, who came from behind her antique desk to shake Theia's hand. "You have no idea how long we've been waiting for you."

"Please, call me Theia."

"Theia. And you must call me Farrah. We had given up all hope of ever finding the artist or any of his descendants. We've been wondering for decades about the artist whose paintings we had possession of and whether anyone would ever claim them. For us, it was one of the great mysteries of the twentieth century, like the disappearance of Amelia Earhart or the assassination of JFK or where the body of Jimmy Hoffa is buried. To date, we've not been able to do anything about this amazing discovery. We've had Chagall scholars researching the artist's paintings. They are so amazing, so alive, so hopeful, and they've been hidden away in our vaults all these years where no one could appreciate them. I hope they're finally going to see the light of day."

Theia didn't want to appear too anxious, although she felt a little lightheaded. She hadn't eaten anything since the lukewarm breakfast served on the flight. "M-may I see them?" she asked tentatively.

"Of course. Let me take you down to the vaults where they're stored. Have you ever seen any of your grandfather's paintings?"

"No," said Theia. "I was led to understand that most of them were destroyed during the war."

"Well, fortunately, Marc Chagall and his daughter had the foresight to bring them to us to have them preserved until the artist could come to collect them. If for no other reason, your grandfather's paintings have incalculable historic value, not to mention monetary value. We've been dying to know more, or even anything, about this artist Theo Frangos and how he came to be associated with Chagall. We had all but given up hope, and then you called."

Perhaps Farrah was nervous, the way she was chattering on, but it was difficult for Theia to concentrate on what the curator was saying. Still lightheaded, Theia steadied herself before she fainted dead away.

"Theia, you look a little pale. Sit down here. Have you had anything to eat or drink today?"

"No, I flew in yesterday and slept, but I really haven't eaten anything. I think it's just low blood sugar."

Farrah reached into her desk drawer, then handed Theia a candy bar. "We're on the run here, so we often don't get regular meals. This is from my secret stash."

Theia stripped off the wrapper, bit into the nutty-chocolate candy, and sighed. Farrah excused herself, stepped across the hall to a break room, and brought back a bottle of fruit juice. Theia downed the whole bottle at once.

"I must have been dehydrated."

Farrah took the candy wrapper and the empty bottle from Theia and took them back to the break room.

"And now, what you've been waiting for—really, what we've all been waiting for."

She led Theia to a bank of elevators, and they went down, stopping on a lower floor where Theia followed her into a temperature-controlled room with an open area in the middle.

"Your grandfather's paintings stand on their own as magnificent examples of a personal style that frankly is indefinable," Farrah said. "His style was influenced by Chagall, of course—part impressionism, post-impressionism, and realism. But his work is unique, and we would classify him as one of the great modern artists. As you'll see, his imagery is whimsical, with a dreamlike quality. Just as Chagall's paintings were reminiscent of his native village of Vitebsk in Belorussia, your grandfather used what we are calling 'Crete Scenes' as his inspiration, especially scenes of Chania. I have displayed the paintings over here so you can get a feel for his entire body of work. According to our records, he spent a year in southern France with Chagall. He must have painted feverishly during that period. I think this probably calls for a drum roll." She stepped aside to let Theia study the paintings.

When Theia set eyes on the display, she wept. "Sorry, Miss Stone…um, Farrah."

"I'm sure you're overwhelmed. Like Chagall often

painted his first wife, Bella, your grandfather seemed to favor a particular model as his subject."

"That would be my grandmother, Eleni," Theia said, marveling at how Ya-Ya seemed to come alive on the canvas. It was as if she were right here in the room with her.

"The model looks a lot like you, in fact," Farrah pointed out.

"People say I favor her."

Theia paced the makeshift display with wonder. The paintings depicted slices of life in Greece, in the background, whitewashed buildings, splashed with crystal seas of various shades of blue and green: the artist's own wedding scene, scenes with Eleni alone, scenes at the beach, scenes of families, of everyday people doing everyday tasks—hanging laundry, working in shops, eating in restaurants—a vibrant community, in a style reminiscent of Chagall but also unique. Then there was the artist's French period, scenes in the south of France.

"They're magnificent," whispered Theia as she approached one of the paintings. She touched her grandfather's signature—Theo Frangos. It was the closest she was going to get to the artist, the man. If things had been different, she might have been born in Crete, lived her life there.

Theo's "Crete Scenes" were realistic yet had a fairytale quality. Theia recognized the Venetian Harbour of Chania, the Venetian Lighthouse, and views of the Old Port of Chania, which evoked memories of her moonlight strolls with Wade in Old Town after a delicious dinner. There were marvelous views from the fortress on top of Gramvousa, narrow cobblestone alleyways, quaint street scenes, a fish stall, Balos Lagoon, landmarks, a shipwreck, grazing sheep. So his memories of Crete had not been obliterated.

The curator was beyond excited, and her energy was contagious. "We have to show these as soon as possible. Imagine, they've been sitting in this vault since Marc Chagall left them during the war. We thought, or rather hoped, there were more of this man's paintings out in the world. But it seems that's not the case. Could you fill me in on the artist's life?"

"Yes, certainly. I will tell you what I know." Theia communicated as much as she could remember of what she had learned from Sophia in the synagogue in Crete. When she got to the sinking of the *Tanais*, the curator was almost in tears.

"And there are letters, letters from the artist to his wife, my grandmother."

"They would be priceless," said Farrah. "The paintings are priceless."

"I've made copies of the letters and brought them to you. Will you put the paintings up for sale?" Theia wondered.

"That would be entirely up to you. Our hope is that you'll allow us to put together a retrospective exhibition of the artist's work."

"An exhibition? Isn't that every artist's dream? I would love that for him."

"Are you an artist?"

"Yes. Though I never knew my grandfather or ever saw one of his paintings, our styles are similar."

Farrah's hand flew to her heart. "We have to explore this. I'm picturing a display of his paintings with his letters, perhaps some photographs if you have them, and information about the life of the artist."

"I've left the photographs in Crete, but I'm sure I can arrange to have them sent over for the exhibition. I will have to talk to my mother, but I think she would be agreeable. I'd like to have her fly up right away to see her father's paintings."

"I would love to meet her," Farrah said.

"Ever since I made the pilgrimage to Crete I have imagined a scene depicting the tragedy of the *Tanais*. I would like to paint it. If it turns out the way I imagine it, the way I hope it will, and it is up to your standards, perhaps it could be part of the exhibition."

"It will be a welcome addition," Farrah assured her. "What exactly did you have in mind?"

"I envision a large horizontal canvas, similar in size to Picasso's *Guernica*, so I will need a studio. I thought I'd stay in New York and paint. Do you have any recommendations for space and an apartment I could rent?"

"I have in mind just the place. It's across from the Frick on East Seventieth Street. A beautiful, quiet neighborhood. Your use of the space would be complimentary. We have an apartment set aside for our visiting artists, and it's currently available. I believe you'll find the accommodations comfortable and the surroundings inspirational. And one of the rooms is already set up as a studio. Let me write down the address. How soon can you move in?"

"I'd like to take occupancy right away and start on the project. I'll probably need it for at least three months."

"That will work out perfectly as far as timing. We have a lot of work to do to complete the exhibition.

That way you can be close by so we can collaborate."

****

Theia and Farrah parted ways, and Theia called her mother. Carolina agreed to take the first flight out from Atlanta to New York City.

After a tearful reunion with her mother, in which Theia explained everything she had learned, the two wept again when they spent the day at MOMA looking at Theo's paintings. Theia's plan was to spend the next three months locked in her studio to complete the new painting and work with the museum curator on the catalogue that would accompany the special exhibition.

She planned to invite members of the six families —those of the five children from Crete Eleni had managed to save, plus her own family. The survivors should be there. It was part of their legacy. The curator had agreed to display family pictures and, in pride of place, the wedding portrait of Ya-Ya and the artist. The photographs on the Memory Wall in Crete would be on loan for the exhibition. She would be so busy she wouldn't have time to think about Wade. Maybe the ache in her heart would eventually subside.

Chapter Thirteen

Theia started by sketching a series of preliminary drawings—studies. Picasso had allowed visitors into his studio to watch him paint. Theia did not favor letting people see her work in progress. It was too intense. When she was working she couldn't afford to lose her focus.

She had to get this right. She had to do this alone. Nothing could interrupt, not yearning or love. Because she did love Wade. How had that happened? No matter, she couldn't fulfill her destiny with him. Ya-Ya had always been such a force in her life. What would Ya-Ya say if she were here right now? Probably that meeting Wade was fate. And fate can't be controlled. But Ya-Ya wasn't here.

So back to the painting. She began by thinking about what colors she would use. She'd envisioned her creation would be colorful. But even the selection of color involved a number of decisions. Cool colors? Warm colors? And there were warm and cool versions of each color. Ultramarine? Cerulean Blue? Cadmium or Lemon Yellow? Colors could not be viewed in isolation. They were selected for impact by how they related to and contrasted with other colors. And that would have to be determined by the story she wanted to tell.

All the colors of the spectrum were available to

her: violet, indigo, blue, green, yellow, orange, and red, but artist's pigments are not absolute like the colors of the rainbow, and she could mix almost any color under the sun from three primary colors. Adding black and white would only increase the range of possibilities. How would she use the neutral colors, the grays, the beiges, the browns, the greenish-grays as a successful framework for the brighter colors? Such necessary considerations occupied her mind before she ever started mixing colors.

The museum had sent over a large horizontal piece of linen fabric, stretched over wood, perfectly framed and squared off to her specifications. The canvas had been pulled from top to bottom and left to right and from the middle, until it was even. It was an important size for an important painting. She then primed it with gesso tinted with an undercoat of color.

Theia's habit was to sketch the picture first before she mixed the colors or even picked up a paintbrush. She had all of her materials: her starter palette—kidney-shaped and made of wood—traditional oils, linseed oil to thin out the paint, turpentine, and the round and other shaped and sized brushes. She particularly preferred the broad, flat brushes, especially for strokes of thick, light paint to capture a sweeping sky, and one or two soft brushes used for small details. With such a large canvas, she would have to lay down little sections at a time, starting with a graphite sketch. Painting materials were not cheap, but the museum very generously supplied anything her painter's heart desired. They were making a big investment in her, and she was not going to disappoint them.

She had already decided on an oil painting on

canvas. The oil paint was thick and creamy; it would hold the marks or strokes of the brush very well, and as any artist knew, brushwork was integral to the painting. Oils could be used straight from the tube. Consistency in brushwork and approach throughout the process was as important as how to mix the colors, getting the drawing right, and depicting her subject.

So for colors... According to her ya-ya's letters, the sun shines brighter, the sky is clearer, the sea is bluer, the fruit is sweeter, and the fish is fresher in Greece. She wanted to show those qualities.

Guernica had been kept for safekeeping at the Museum of Modern Art in New York City in 1981 before it was returned to Spain that same year, and Theia was proud her painting would also be housed in the Museum of Modern Art.

During the Spanish Civil War, the Luftwaffe had bombed the village of Guernica for about two hours, a precursor of the Blitzkrieg. It had taken the *Tanais* only fifteen minutes to sink. The victims were mostly women and children. How would she portray the lost children of Chania? Should her painting be similar to *Guernica* in the emotions it elicited?

Saying the Jews were lost made it sound like they were some misplaced tribe in the Amazon that had gone missing. They weren't missing; they had been *murdered*. There was no other way to say it. From the moment she'd learned about the *Tanais*, she'd been angry. But anger wasn't fueling her creativity, it was stifling it. Lately, her sleep had been interrupted with ghoulish dreams of drowning, torture, hardship, helplessness, and grief.

Theia alternately stared up at the humongous,

essentially blank canvas and the crumpled sketches in the trash can. She was too overwhelmed to start.

She continued to sketch all day and in the middle of the night woke up sweating, her heart pounding, parched, desperate for a drink of clean water. The room was closing in. She imagined herself trapped with hundreds of desperate people in the cramped hold of the ship, unable to see sunlight or reach the deck, strangling for a breath of fresh air, and then the torpedoes blasted open the hull of the boat with two mind-numbing explosions, and there came the agony of drowning in a deep, murky sea scattered with unrecognizable, floating body parts and the muffled cries of yearning souls.

When she awoke, she gulped in the fresh air as she threw off the cumbersome covers. It was like she was reliving the tragedy of the *Tanais*. Her grandfather's spirit had possessed her, filling her mind with how it must have felt during those last desperate moments. She went into the bathroom and wiped the moisture off her body with a towel before she took a large glass of water to ward off her feelings of dread.

Another nightmare. When she had had them at the hotel in Florence, Wade had been there to hold her. But Wade wasn't here now because she had pushed him away.

The very idea of the project was intimidating. She imagined being confronted with the desolate glare of white-on-white was like a novelist staring at a blank, flickering screen on a computer, wondering how to start a story. She wasn't just painting for herself but for her family, for the grandfather she'd never known, whose life had been cut short, for the memory of the grandmother she loved, and for the lost souls of Chania.

She spent the day circling the room, trying to come to terms with the canvas. The next day, she tried strolling around Central Park and visiting the Frick, which was lovely, but it was even more intimidating to see all that talent on display—old masters and nineteenth-century paintings from Rembrandt and El Greco to Goya, Vermeer, and Fragonard. What an ego-buster. She was certain she was going to disappoint everyone. Why had she ever agreed to this? How could she paint the destruction of an entire community? How would she not wallow in grief when she undertook such a daunting task? How could she capture the victims' despair?

Theia paced the condo. She looked out the window onto East 70th Street. It was a quiet haven, away from the hustle and bustle of the city. The morning sunlight spilled through the studio window. And suddenly she had a breakthrough. Maybe her approach was all wrong. Instead of imitating Picasso's grim portrayal of universal suffering of the innocent victims of war, Theia's work should be uplifting, hopeful. Maybe the painting should be more of a tribute, not a condemnation. Gradually her mind began to clear. She went to the coffee table in the living room, where she had a book about Chagall, and that was where she got her inspiration—from her grandfather's mentor.

Could it be her grandfather's spirit was speaking to her? She was approaching the piece all wrong. This painting didn't have to be anything like *Guernica*. It didn't have to depict children going down at sea to a dark watery grave, and victims trapped in a hot, stuffy hold, unsure of what fate awaited them at their destination. No, in her version of the tragedy, they would escape their fate, their souls flying into heaven to be snatched up at the last minute by a protective angel. She would depict every one of the two hundred and sixty-five Jews, including the one hundred lost children, mothers with their children, lovers clinging to each other for the last time, and her grandfather, the artist. Now that she understood the message, this painting would be one of hope. The only ones going down with the ship would be the Germans, in leg irons and Nazi uniforms, fear frozen on their ghoulish faces.

The souls would mount upward, swooping heavenward. Maybe she would call it *Jews of Chania Take Flight*. It would not be inspired by Picasso's *Guernica*. Instead she would infuse it with hope—no screams, agonized wails, or choking. Instead, it would teem with life and hope. It would be her ancestors' final journey, to paradise.

The color combinations began forming in her mind. In the background were the mountains, the blue and white colors depicting Greece. Her grandfather would be shown, holding out hope that his beloved and their child had been spared, rescued, and that he would see them again in heaven. Each of the two hundred and sixty-five souls would be individually rendered, drawn from the research and photos of the families that had perished. Now she knew why she had snapped copies of those photos. In her heart, she knew this was a picture her grandfather would have painted, had he lived, one he wanted her to paint, as he had communicated to her in dreams. Babies in nappies, children safe in their mothers' arms, lovers staring into each others' souls.

Picasso had painted *Guernica* in thirty-five days. Plagued with doubts, she had to face the fact that she was no Picasso. She wasn't even an experienced painter. She'd never painted on such a large canvas before or for such an important audience. What made her think any painting of hers would be worthy of an exhibition? But she was determined to work day and night and complete her painting in only one more day than the master—thirty-six days, double Chai or eighteen, a spiritual number in Judaism—in honor of the Jews who had lost their lives.

She'd always been drawn to Chagall, and now she knew why. She would paint in the tradition for which Chagall was known, to honor him, but with her grandfather's touch and her own unique style. She captured these ideas and others in her mind, then refined her key figures in sketch after sketch, which she would rework several times before she transferred the sketches to the canvas.

She would portray the drowning victims, especially the children, as cherubic angels floating toward heaven, each safe in its mother's arms. Truly, they were headed for a better place than their original destination, almost certain death in the concentration camps.

Theia's work would be all about color and joy. She would call it *The Ascending Souls of Chania*.

She would paint the scene her grandfather saw in his final minutes, a scene he had no way of painting. His spirit had imbued her with his vision, and he was working through her like a writer's characters spoke to the author from the cosmos, urging them to put their feelings into words on the page. Her grandfather was channeling through her. Her fingers were electrified, her mind aflame. She was driven to complete this painting.

The paintings she had seen of her grandfather's in the museum vault were not horrifying. That was what she was had been doing wrong. Those paintings were light and hopeful and full of color.

Theia got out her paints and her palette. Suddenly she saw the finished work in her mind's eye, and she worked feverishly to achieve that vision.

With a blue background, she painted the ship before it had been blown to bits by the torpedoes. The unwilling passengers had escaped this life and were on their way to a better place before their ship had even been sighted.

Babies swaddled in pink and blue blankets, cradled in their mothers' arms, heartbeats synchronized until their final beat when they ascended to heaven, each with a set of strong wings, fluttering up to a cornflower-blue sky with wisps of billowing white clouds. Husbands and wives, clinging to each other, love in their eyes, because they knew when they got to their destination they would be united forever. Families, hand in hand with their children.

It was the middle of the night on rough seas, but in her painting, the full moon would illuminate the sky, kissing the waves. There was no utter darkness, no debilitating final moments of fear and hopelessness, no lurking submarine lying in wait. Only smiling faces, looking upward toward the bright light.

And, in pride of place, her grandfather, Theo, larger than life, magnificent angel wings unfurled, leading the way. Yes, that is how she wanted to remember him. How she wanted the world to remember him. The stars rode high in the sky, especially one shining star, representing her grandmother.

Swirls of color—yellows, greens, and blues. The painting was wild, Impressionistic. Her interpretation of events would be hopeful.

She worked through the night, and when she finally slept, she slept peacefully for the first time since her trip abroad, uninterrupted by bad dreams or night sweats.

She woke up the next day, painted some more, painting until her hands were raw. But she definitely had something, at least the beginnings of something, something original, something she could be proud of, something she thought Theo would be proud of.

At night, she lay still and quiet in bed, in her summer nightgown, the only sound being the air conditioner cycling on and off. Eventually, she drifted off to sleep.

During the days, she didn't go out for sustenance. She ordered in. Shut off from the world, albeit by her choice, she lived with her fears and insecurities. What if she weren't good enough to tell the story the way it needed to be told? What made her think she had the talent to bring the tragedy to life? She was not her grandfather.

Then one of her brothers called.

"T, some dude named Wade dropped by asking about you, wondering where you are and when you're coming home."

"He actually came to the house? What did you tell him?"

"Nothing, just like you told us to say. But this guy seems like he's on the level. He's really hurting. I think you broke his heart."

"That's ridiculous," Theia said. "We hardly know

each other."

"That's not what he said."

"What did he say, exactly?"

"It's not what he said, but how he said it. Why don't you give him a break?"

"I can't focus on anyone or anything until I finish this painting. I'm facing a deadline, and I'm not making enough progress."

"Maybe you're too caught up in it. Relax and maybe things will look different. Meanwhile, can I give the guy your address so he can visit, or at least your phone number? He's called every one of us, including Mom and Dad."

"No, you can't. I'm sorry, but I have to finish this project."

"He says he's not Greek."

"He's not."

"Or Jewish."

"That's right, he's neither of these."

"And that that's the reason you broke up with him, as if any of that mattered if you love the guy. That's just plain crazy. Welcome to the twenty-first century. You're free to do whatever you want."

"Then how come you and all of my brothers are dating or married to Greek girls?"

"That's all we know. We've been around them all our lives, in synagogue, school, hanging out with the children of Mom and Dad's friends."

"I rest my case."

"Do you love him?" her brother asked.

Theia was quiet. She had given it enough thought all these weeks—months, really—alone.

"Yes."

"Then I really don't get it. I'll tell him you're as stubborn as a mule's mother-in-law and once you make up your mind, you never change it, and what does he see in you anyway."

"Thanks."

Her brother's voice was serious. "T, I've been elected to tell you that we all miss you. We're here for you, if you'd only reach out."

"Thanks, but I have to do this myself. Finishing this painting is my top priority."

"Mom wants to talk to you."

"Putting on the big guns?"

"Yep."

She said goodbye to her brother.

"Hi, honey," said Carolina. "I like your young man. We all do."

"He's not my young man."

"He could be."

"He's not Greek."

"What does that matter? It's obvious he loves you. Don't turn your back on love. It's a gift from God."

"You don't even know him."

Carolina was silent.

"He doesn't live in Atlanta. It would never work out."

"He said actuaries can work anywhere."

"Are you his agent or a matchmaker?"

"No, I'm your mother, and I don't want you to make a mistake."

"It's not a mistake. I'm too busy painting. I don't have time for a relationship."

"We miss you."

"I miss you all too. I'm looking forward to seeing

you all at the exhibition." She broke the connection with her mother, possessed and eager to get back to her project.

Theia worked day and night, almost without a break. She subsisted on minimal meals and rarely dined out. And, miraculously, thirty-six days after she started, the end was in sight.

She wanted to shout. She wanted to call someone. She wanted—no needed—to talk to Wade. She'd thought about calling him many times since she'd arrived in New York, but each time she stopped herself. He had been part of her journey, and she had sent him an invitation to the exhibition. She didn't have much time to miss him during the day, but she did in fact miss him fiercely in the quiet hours of the evening.

She sat on the bed and dialed his number.

He answered on the first ring, like he'd been waiting by the phone.

"Hey," she said.

"Hay is for horses."

Theia laughed, for the first time in a long time. "You're a dork. You know that, don't you?"

"You haven't talked to me in more than a month, and that's the best you can come up with?"

"Sorry." She smiled through the phone. "It's good to hear your voice."

"Theia, I want more than to hear your voice. I *need* to see you."

Theia exhaled.

"Don't shut me out," Wade implored.

"I just called to tell you that I'm done."

"Done with me?"

"No, done with the painting, silly. Well, I still have

to add the finishing touches. I am almost ready to put my signature on it. I'm sorry I wouldn't let you visit, but I was so caught up. I lost my way at first, but then I had a breakthrough, and I've been painting day and night. Did you get my invitation to the opening?"

"Not yet."

"Well, I put your name on the list. I'd like you to come to New York for the reception. I was afraid I'd lost you."

"I'm still yours to lose," Wade said. "I'd go anywhere for you, Theia. Just name the place and time."

She gave him the details.

"I can't wait. See you soon, then, love," Wade added.

Theia hung up the phone and sighed. He'd called her "love." If there was such a thing as floating on air, then she was weightless. She flipped herself backward on the bed and imagined Wade was there with her. What would it be like when she saw him again after all this time? She couldn't wait.

Like a caged tiger, Theia paced the length of the apartment, anxious for a new day to dawn. The next morning, she walked to Sarabeth's at Central Park South and had a big breakfast. She started with a glass of Four Flowers Juice, with orange, fresh pineapple, banana, and pomegranate juice, followed by Fat & Fluffy French Toast and a basket of muffins to take back to the apartment.

Her clothes were hanging on her. She had been thin to begin with, and now none of her clothes fit. It hadn't mattered, because she painted in an old T-shirt, a T-shirt she'd stolen from Wade's luggage before she left for New York. It was still infused with Wade's manly smell. It was what had sustained her all these weeks.

She needed to go shopping for a perfect dress for the opening. And she was in the right town to do her shopping. She stuck the bag with the muffins into her purse and stopped into Sak's couture department. Browsing through the designer gowns, she settled on a Carmen Marc Valvo floor-length chiffon gown with a beaded neck. Its pattern looked like a palette Monet could have painted, streaked with hot pink, royal blue, green, gray, blue-green accent flowers arrayed on a white background. It was flowy and tied at the waist in a simple bow. She took a cab back to drop off her packages and spent the rest of the day walking through the park, finally taking in the sights and sounds of New York City. It felt good to walk and to stretch. To have accomplished something she was proud of.

When she got back to her apartment, she called the curator at the museum.

"I finished," said Theia, the relief obvious in her voice. "Well, except for a few touchups, and then it needs to dry. You can come take a look, if you'd like."

"You know I've been dying to see it," said Farrah. "And I have the proofs for the brochure to show you."

"How is planning coming for the reception?"

"Everything is going great. We've already received a lot of RSVPs. It's going to be a full event, with your family and friends, our donors, the board, and the media. The response has been overwhelming. The Greek Consul General in New York is coming, *and* the Consul from Atlanta."

Farrah came to the apartment the next day. Theia drew her into her studio, set up in the second bedroom.

Because she was on the fiftieth floor, there was plenty of light, thanks to the open spaces beyond the windows. Theia unveiled the painting, and Farrah just stood there, open-mouthed.

"What do you think?"

"I'm speechless. Theia, I had no idea. It's amazing. It's a masterpiece. I didn't know that you...I mean...I thought...I mean I'd hoped..."

"You had no idea what to expect. It could have been a complete disaster, right?"

Farrah laughed. "The thought had crossed my mind. But Theia, your style is just like your grandfather's. This is phenomenal. You've taken a tragedy and made it uplifting."

"That was not my original intent," Theia explained. "I started in the direction of *Guernica*, and for days, nothing happened. I had a wastebasket full of useless sketches. Then it came to me in a dream. I think Theo's spirit must have taken hold and painted through me. And when I thought about my grandfather's style, I realized he wouldn't have painted anything so dark."

"It's astounding. I can't stop looking at it. I feel like we need some Champagne to celebrate."

"I could certainly use a drink."

"I'm taking you out to dinner tonight. There will be bubbly. When you're finished with the painting, I'll have it transported to the museum. The space is ready, and all we need to do is frame and hang the paintings. Your help in naming the pieces has been invaluable. What will you call this final piece?"

"I had originally named it *Lost Souls of Chania*," Theia began. "But now I'm thinking more along the lines of *The Spirit of Chania* or *Ascending Souls of*

Chania."

"I like it. *Ascending Souls*. It's perfect."

Farrah handed Theia the catalogue proof. "Here, take a look at this and see what you think. I need to have the photographer come by and shoot your painting for the cover."

The women discussed a number of things in connection with the opening, and after Farrah left, Theia spent several hours putting the finishing touches on the painting and, finally, adding her signature.

The promised dinner went farther toward cementing their friendship, and they parted with an appointment to meet in a week at the gallery to finalize placement of the painting in the museum.

Chapter Fourteen

When Theia arrived at MOMA, she took the elevator to Farrah's office.

Farrah grasped her hands. "Well, this is it. I can't wait for you to see it! I couldn't be happier with the way the exhibition is turning out. I hope you will be too."

When Theia walked into the space where the exhibition would be housed, the impact was so powerful, she was transported back to Chania. As she entered the first room, her hand flew to her mouth. There, on the walls in front of her, was the whole story in paintings and photographs, assaulting her senses. The first thing she noticed were the colors, the colors of Greece. The whitewashed buildings with a smattering of colors—pale yellow, peach, blue. She was back in Chania and could feel the warmth and the spirit of the city, could almost soak up the atmosphere. She saw again the Venetian Harbour, the old port, the maze of narrow side streets, the souvenir and arts and craft shops, the Greek tavernas. There was the synagogue with the Memorial Wall, and there on the walls were the actual pictures, borrowed for the exhibit. On the white wall were the names of the victims of the *Tanais*. She touched her hand to her family's name.

Then she entered a giant room devoted to the featured artist—Theo's breathtaking paintings—

paintings of Chania, the harbor, the markets, the beaches, pictures of Theo and his bride, pictures of her ya-ya as a young girl, the story of their romance and their love blossoming in full color. And then as she wandered into the central room, there on the full expanse of wall was her painting.

Choked up, Theia could hardly move. Farrah came up behind her and held her hand.

"There. There it is, Theia. It's remarkable. I don't think the word 'masterpiece' is too overstated."

Theia expelled a breath and couldn't stop the flow of tears.

"The world will finally see your grandfather's talent and your tribute."

There was a long bench in front of the painting. Farrah helped her over to it.

"I'm overwhelmed. I just wish my ya-ya could have seen this," Theia said.

"She would have been proud, I think," said Farrah. "Your family will be proud."

"You've created a lovely exhibition," Theia said. "Thank you."

"No, thank you. Without you, none of this would have been possible."

"And now, for the final surprise." Farrah handed Theia a finished full-color, high-gloss catalogue.

There was her painting on the cover of the brochure, with her name. And in the following pages, pictures of each painting, with explanations, history, and background of the last Jewish community of Chania. The descriptive narrative was supplemented with pictures of the six children who had fled the island all those years ago, and their descendants. There was a section about the artist and his wife, her grandmother.

The curator had asked a Chagall scholar to write a monograph on Theo's paintings. He had been allowed to preview the artist's works before the exhibition opening, and he was excited to discover what he thought was a gifted painter to introduce to the world.

The catalogue created to accompany the exhibition had a table of contents, an acknowledgement written by Theia, a preface, an essay written by the Chagall scholar, photos of artworks in the exhibition, plus other photos provided by Theia, a checklist of the artworks in the exhibition, a bibliography, and an index. The booklet also contained artist monographs or thematic texts by named authors.

Theia smiled. She couldn't wait for her family to arrive for the exhibition. It was the longest she'd ever gone without seeing them, even with her mother's quick visit when she'd first arrived in New York City. She had given so much time to the project, so much of herself, time away from everyone she loved, including Wade. She had come to realize she was in love with Wade. He had gone on the journey of discovery with her. Would he take the next step?

After discussing it with her mother, Theia had gifted Theo's paintings to the museum's permanent collection. She had already decided to donate all the profits from the exhibition to the Etz Hayyim synagogue on Crete, to ensure its future.

****

All her brothers, all her aunts and uncles, and representatives of the other five families were expected at the exhibition, and they all showed up. So did the Greek Consul General in New York, the Greek Consul from Atlanta, and the mayor of Chania, who flew in for the occasion. Sophia was too old to travel, but she had promised to be there in spirit. A videographer had been hired to document the event.

A shiver went down Theia's spine, and when she looked up, Wade was standing at the entrance to the gallery. She'd been watching for him, afraid he wouldn't come, but here he was. The pain of missing Theia was etched on his face. She wanted to run to him and feel his arms around her, but they had an audience. A big audience. An important audience. The reunion would have to wait. She motioned him over.

"Theia," he exhaled, his face beaming. "Finally! I've missed you terribly." He enfolded her in his arms. Then he took a step back and looked at her. "You're as beautiful as ever, but you've lost weight."

"I was so focused, sometimes I forgot to eat. Come, let me show you what I've been doing all this time." She shepherded Wade through the exhibition's rooms.

"Look at this!" Wade exclaimed. "It's like we're back in Chania—the stars in the night sky, the tavernas, the harbor. It feels so real. Is it real? Are you really here? I think I'm dreaming."

"It's not a dream," Theia answered. "Or I'm having the same dream."

As they walked through the exhibition, Wade shook his head. "I had no idea," he said. "These paintings are amazing."

And when he stood in front of hers, tears sparkled in his eyes. "This is yours?"

Theia blushed. "Yes."

"It's as if your grandfather was working through

you. You are a major talent."

"Thank you."

"I've seen your sketches, but I had no idea. It's brilliant. You're brilliant. You belong to the world now, but I want you to belong to me."

Wade took Theia in his arms again. "I missed you. You have no idea." Then he cleared his throat and got down on one knee.

Theia's mouth opened. "Wade, what are you doing?"

"This may not be the time or the place, but I'm more sure now than ever. Theia Constas, I may not be Greek or Jewish, but I am in love with you. I want to spend the rest of my life with you. Will you marry me?"

Theia started crying. "You hardly know me or my family. I mean, I know you met them, but…"

"Now there's where you're wrong. Your family and I have become very well acquainted in your absence. And all I need to know about you is that I love you."

Theia took Wade's hands and lifted him up.

"Wait," Wade said. "I have a ring."

Theia's eyes opened wide.

Wade handed her a velvet box, and her hands shook when she opened it. The ring sparkled under the artificial lights of the chandeliers.

"It's an emerald to match your eyes, but it doesn't do you justice."

"Wade, it's absolutely beautiful. It must have cost a fortune."

"You are worth every penny I spent on it."

He slipped the ring onto her finger, and she held her hand up to the light. "This thing is huge."

"I'm glad you like it."

"I love it." Theia stumbled over the words, all the words she wanted to say to Wade, but all she could manage was, "I love you."

From the broad smile on Wade's face, she knew she had found the right words.

"I've been thinking," Wade started. "I want to take you back to Crete. Let's hold the wedding at the Etz Hayyim synagogue. And for our honeymoon we'll go to all the places we missed the first time—Rome, Capri, Venice, and of course the rest of the Greek islands."

"What a wonderful idea. It's perfect."

"So is that a yes?"

"Yes," she said, melting into Wade's arms.

Theia's parents and brothers came over to them. They hugged Wade.

"Have you asked her yet?" Carolina wanted to know.

"You knew about this, Mom?"

"I helped him pick out the ring. But to answer your question, yes, we had nothing but time, waiting for you. We've gotten to know Wade quite well."

"And you approve?"

"Of course," Carolina said. "He's a fine young man."

"He's not Greek," Theia stated flatly.

"No, but does he make you happy?"

Theia flashed her new engagement ring. "Completely." Then she asked her mother, "Do you think Ya-Ya would approve?"

"Absolutely. I think she was the one who brought you together."

Each member of the family took a turn

congratulating the happy couple.

Carolina had one more thing to say. "He doesn't have to be Greek, but I am expecting a houseful of grandchildren, sooner rather than later." She narrowed her eyebrows at Wade.

"I'm ready to do my duty, Mrs. Constas," stated Wade. "Bring it on. All of it. I can't wait to start my life with your beautiful, amazing, talented daughter."

Wade winked at Theia and pulled her closer. She thought she'd melt right on the spot.

"We need to get moving with the wedding plans, or you're going to turn up pregnant under the chuppah," he said.

"You know what a chuppah is?"

"I've been studying."

"Impressive."

"I mean it, Theia," Wade whispered in her ear. "I really can't wait. I've booked us a suite at the Shoreham, a luxury boutique hotel nearby. Our room is stocked with Champagne and flowers and chocolates, in hopes that you would say yes."

He circled her wrist with his fingers. "You haven't been eating properly. That's all going to change. I'll have to fatten you up, not that I'm complaining. I planned a big celebration for us. And now that you've said yes, I'm anxious to get an early start on making that family your mom was talking about. I don't intend to disappoint her or you."

Theia blushed. It had been a long time since they'd made love. Too long. She was more than ready to feel Wade's body next to hers, to feel him inside her, to walk hand in hand with him around the city, to share a meal, to share a bed, to fill the empty places in her heart. They were both on the same page. She tugged on his jacket shyly, impatience and longing reflected in her eyes. He turned to face her.

Theia rose up on her tiptoes and threw her arms around Wade's neck as he planted a flurry of soft, slow, wet kisses on her lips that left her wanting more.

"I'm eager too, sweetheart. That will have to do for now, but shouldn't we wait a respectable amount of time before we leave? After all, you're the star of the show."

"What I have in mind, Mr. Bingham, is not respectable. What are the odds that we make it out of here in the next five minutes?"

Wade groaned. "I'd say the odds are in our favor."

Chapter Fifteen

Wade and Theia stood, hands clasped, under the chuppah in the Etz Hayyim synagogue. The rabbi had flown in from Athens to conduct the ceremony. Theia's family and Wade's family had flown in to Chania, and all the Constas friends and relatives had shown up for the destination wedding. Sophia was there.

The photographer shot views of the bride and groom in their formal wear. Theia looked like a goddess. She wore her hair parted in the middle and pulled back, held in place with flowers, and she was a vision in her Christos Costarellos gown from the Greek fashion designer's Spring Wedding Dress Collection. Wade's sister, who was a fashion consultant for a San Francisco department store, had helped her pick it out. How could he describe the gown? How could he describe his bride? She was a fantasy in what seemed to him to be layers and layers of multiple laces and tulle in a feminine banded-waist ball gown.

According to his sister, Theia had selected that gown because the designer was a Greek native and because of his attention to detail and quality fabrics and his trendy yet uniquely Mediterranean style. She had discovered new details in each fitting, right up until the wedding day. He could see her in this refined gown on a fashion runway or running barefoot on the beach. In fact, the photographer went crazy transporting the wedding party all over the island, to shoot them at this beach and that, in front of some sailboats, and in the harbor.

A copy of their best wedding photo would hang on the Memory Wall, right next to the wedding photo of Theo and Eleni. There was plenty of empty space for Bingham baby pictures. Wade wanted six children. That was fine with Theia.

Wade and Theia recited their vows, exchanged rings, and clung to each other for the kiss.

"Hey, T, save some for the honeymoon," one of her brothers shouted.

"Remember where you are, T," said another.

Then there was the inevitable, "Get a room!" from another brother.

****

Theia could take all the ribald ribbing. That's what brothers were like. That's what family was like. She couldn't wait to build a family with Wade. The sun shone down and the sea sparkled in the distance like diamonds. The festivities continued under a tent in the synagogue courtyard. There were flowers everywhere, and dancing, music, and more food than she'd ever seen in her life. Sophia's friends had been baking for weeks.

She felt Ya-Ya's presence, and Theo's too. Wade's idea for them to marry in the same place as her grandparents had been inspired.

She looked up at Wade with eyes of love. She was sure she had made the right decision and that she had married the right man. She couldn't wait for the honeymoon. They would spend the night at a secluded bed and breakfast on the island, then board a cruise to the rest of the islands. After that, Wade insisted on taking her to Rome, Capri, and Venice, to visit churches and museums to her heart's content. She would sketch, and then paint the scenes they encountered once she got back home.

They planned to stay on the continent for a month and fly out through Paris so Theia could visit the Louvre and other museums in that city, too. Wade knew what a hometown girl she was and how close she was to her parents. So they would settle in Atlanta, where Wade had already found a new job. But it didn't matter where they lived. As long as they were together, they would be home. They had bought a big house and were anxious to begin the project of filling it with children.

"Are you happy, Mrs. Bingham?" Wade asked when they were able to grab a minute alone. He hated to share her and couldn't wait to get her alone and out of her spectacular wedding dress.

Breathless from dancing, she replied, "Deliriously, Mr. Bingham."

"What were the odds that you and I would end up together?" Wade wondered.

"I think fate brought us together. My ya-ya sent me on this trip hoping I'd find a husband, and I did. I think she would approve of you."

"I hope so. I hope we're as happy as Theo and Eleni were when they started out their lives together, and I calculate we will have a long and happy life."

Acknowledgments

Thanks to Dr. Morris "Mo" Soriano for sharing his family's story about their emigration to Atlanta from Rhodes and his memories of his subsequent visits to Rhodes and of the Sephardic Jewish community in Atlanta.

For more information about the unique history of the Jews of Rhodes, there is a wonderful site that chronicles a historical exhibition, located in the rooms formerly used as the women's prayer rooms at the Kahal Shalom synagogue, which is now The Jewish Museum of Rhodes:

http://www.rhodesjewishmuseum.org/

~

How did *The Siege* come about? I created this story long after my husband and I visited Athens and the Greek islands, including Crete and Rhodes. On Rhodes, I met a woman Mo says was named Lucia, a Holocaust survivor who came to the temple every day to relate the story of the Jews of Rhodes while she was alive. She is similar to the elderly man I met at Dachau (who has surely passed on by now) who also volunteered his time daily at the former concentration camp to tell the story to those who came to visit. Lucia is the inspiration for my character Sophia.

On Rhodes, I remember seeing a Memory Wall of sorts, with photos sent from locations around the globe, from Jewish families who left the Greek island before the Holocaust and flourished. While we were there, I distinctly remember seeing the name Soriano as one of the families who emigrated. I knew that family from Atlanta.

Somehow, I got the two islands confused. While there also was a synagogue on Crete, I thought I remembered hearing the docent tell me about six children who left the island at the start of the war and so were saved from certain death at the hands of the Germans. They started families of their own around the world, keeping the Jewish tradition of Crete alive.

According to Mo, there were five families on Rhodes who left long before the war, in the 1920s, for primarily economic reasons. Whatever the reasons, they signify the fact that the Jews did manage to survive World War II even though there are only a handful left on each island.

When I found out the tragic true story of the *Tanais,* which had happened to the Jews of Crete, I thought I had my story. After I interviewed Mo, I found that I had blurred the stories of the two islands. But I decided to keep my story set on Crete, which had an interesting World War II history of its own.

~

Mo told me about his Congregation Or Ve Shalom's sisterhood that makes Turkish turnover pastries called burekas—a Jewish Sephardic dish that has been handed down from generation to generation. They bake the light and flaky dough with love and five fillings—potato, spinach, rice, eggplant, and ground beef—as a ritual every Tuesday morning and sell them by the dozen as a fundraiser, along with desserts they sell at their annual Hanukkah Bazaar. To get these savory hand-held pies, email:

orderburekas@orveshalom.org

To find out more about this tradition, watch the podcast "Pie by Another Name—The Burekas of Or Ve Shalom," produced by the Southern Foodways Alliance at:

https://www.southernfoodways.org/gravy/pie-by-another-name-the-burekas-of-or-ve-shalom/

~

The artist Theo Frangos was a figment of my imagination. He never existed. He never studied with Chagall in France. Although who's to say, if there had never been a Holocaust, had never been a *Tanais*, that one of the children on the vessel wouldn't have grown up to be a famous artist? It's possible. And the doomed children didn't have to *be* anything. It would have been enough just to let them exist. The wasted human potential of that time is difficult to imagine.

Thanks to my friend Lisa Frangos Dossey for loaning me her maiden name for my character Theo.

The love story between Theo and Eleni is also fictitious. But they are typical of the couples who fell in love, got married, and were lost in the Holocaust.

A word about the author...

Marilyn Baron writes humorous coming-of-*middle*-age women's fiction, historical romantic thrillers, suspense, and paranormal/fantasy. A public relations consultant in Atlanta, she's a PAN member of Romance Writers of America (RWA) and Georgia Romance Writers (GRW) and winner of the GRW 2009 Chapter Service Award and writing awards in single title, suspense romance, paranormal/fantasy, and novel with strong romantic elements.

She's the Finalist in the 2017 Georgia Author of the Year Awards in the Romance category for *Stumble Stones: A Novel*. She's a member of the 2017-18 Roswell Reads Committee. She graduated from the University of Florida in Gainesville, Florida, with a Bachelor of Science in Journalism (Public Relations sequence) and a minor in Creative Writing.

Born in Miami, Florida, Marilyn lives in Roswell, GA, with her husband, and they have two daughters.

To find out more about Marilyn's books, please visit her Web site at www.marilynbaron.com.